D0192145

LOVING PROTECTOR

En route to London for the Season, Calista Haywood and her family are saved from a highwayman by the dashing Brook Windebank. Later, when he valiantly steps in to prevent an unpleasant earl from claiming Calista as his wife, she fears that Brook is only being chivalrous and will never love her as she loves him. Then, when Brook is attacked and lying close to death, she is forced to pit her wits against his mercurial father, the Duke of Midchester . . .

SALLY QUILFORD

LOVING PROTECTOR

9 013427566

Complete and Unabridged

LINFORD
Leicester

First published in Great Britain in 2013

First Linford Edition
published 2015

*A catalogue record for this book is available
from the British Library.*

ISBN 978–1–4448–2301–1

Published by
F. A. Thorpe (Publishing)
Anstey, Leicestershire

Set by Words & Graphics Ltd.
Anstey, Leicestershire
Printed and bound in Great Britain by
T. J. International Ltd., Padstow, Cornwall

This book is printed on acid-free paper

1

'I do not see why she has to come to London,' said Blanche Kirkham. She glared at her mother and then at Calista. Blanche was tall and beautiful, but with a temper as dark as her hair and eyes.

The coach in which they were travelling rocked over the uneven ground.

'We can hardly leave Calista at home,' said Mrs. Evelyn Haywood. 'As I explained to you, dearest, I could not afford to pay for the upkeep of Haywood Manor and your Season in London.' Evelyn was very much like her daughter in looks, except that her face had softer features, and kind brown eyes.

'I would have been quite happy to stay home, Evelyn,' said Calista, looking up from her book. Polar opposite to her step-sister, Blanche, Calista was petite and pretty, with fair hair and cornflower-blue eyes.

'You say that,' said Blanche, before her mother could answer, 'but I know you will be monopolizing all the men for yourself. As you always do.'

Calista laughed. 'I am not aware I have ever done such a thing, Blanche. They only speak to me when you are not available.'

'She must stay out of the way,' Blanche said to Evelyn. 'If she prefers to stay at home, then she may stay indoors in London. She is much too old for a Season anyway.'

'I am only six months older than you,' said Calista, with a grin that showed pretty dimples in her cheeks.

'Mama, you are not to tell people I am twenty. You are to say I am eighteen.'

'Blanche, dearest, I cannot lie.'

'I shall be telling people I am eighteen and if you contradict me, Mama, it will look very bad for you.' She added waspishly, 'It will make you seem older for a start.'

'Blanche, I am thirty-eight years old

and every one of those years shows on my face. Probably a few more besides. I cannot pretend to be otherwise.'

'I am sure you would look much younger had you married a richer man instead of Bryan Haywood. Poverty makes people older quicker.'

Calista's eyes flashed and she was about to make a retort along the lines that Blanche's real father had been poorer still. She hated to hear the way Blanche spoke about her late father, who had shown Blanche nothing but kindness, despite her many barbed insults to him.

'But I would not have been happier,' said Evelyn.

'Oh Mama, you are so stupid sometimes. If we had money we would be very happy. When I marry a Duke or an Earl, then we will be happy. Calista can go back to her little house and with any luck she may persuade a farmer's son to marry her.'

'I do not see how there would be anything wrong with that if I loved him,' said Calista.

'See?' Blanche gesticulated towards Calista. 'This is the sort of family you have married into mother. She will bring shame on us, I can feel it. Not that it will matter when I am the Duchess. I shall tell people that I have disowned her.'

'Do not count your chickens before they are hatched,' said Calista. 'You have not yet met a Duke or Earl, nor he you.' In truth, Calista had no doubt Blanche would catch the eye of such a man. She was beautiful enough, and could be quite charming when she wanted to be. Added to which, Calista doubted a man from the nobility would be as intimidated by Blanche as the young men who lived in their town.

'Do you see how cruelly she treats me, Mama?' said Blanche, starting to build up to one of her tempers

'But you also treat Calista cruelly,' said Evelyn. 'And I wish you would not. Please try to remember that it is her father's money that is paying for your

Season in London.'

'Sometimes I think you love her more than me,' said Blanche, wiping her eyes, which Calista was interested to note were dry.

'Of course not,' said Evelyn. 'You are my daughter and naturally I love you more.' Evelyn looked at Calista with something like guilt in her eyes. 'But I am also very fond of Calista. She has been a great help to me since her father died.'

'And I have not?'

'Well, no, not really, dear. Not when you insult a man I loved dearly.'

'I am bored with this conversation now. Tell me about the dresses you are going to buy me. I shall need at least two morning dresses and two evening dresses.'

'I am afraid that will not be possible. You and Calista may have one new morning dress and one new evening dress each. Other than that you will have to wear your usual clothes. Calista and I have worked hard to spruce up our old dresses. We will all look very elegant when we are presented to society.'

'Mama! I have told you. She is not to go anywhere. She is to stay indoors with those boring books she reads. She will be quite happy.'

'I know what you have told me, Blanche, but as I have just told you, it is Bryan's money that is paying for this Season. So Calista shall have her pretty dresses too.'

'I hate you!' Blanche raged. 'I hate you, Mother. You have ruined my life. Ruined it.'

Evelyn and Calista exchanged glances. They knew what would come next. Blanche had been building up to it ever since Evelyn had refused to leave Calista at home when they left that morning.

Blanche's tantrum was curtailed. The coach suddenly lurched to a halt and they heard a man shouting, 'Stand and deliver.'

'A highwayman!' said Calista, her heart beating rapidly. Since the end of the Napoleonic Wars, many returning soldiers, having found there was no work for them, had turned to highway robbery.

'I thought they only struck at night,' said Evelyn. They could still hear talking outside, but as yet no one had come to the coach door. 'How far are we from London?'

'About an hour, I think,' said Calista.

'That means help will be a long time coming.'

Blanche had gone very quiet and very white in the face. Her hands trembled. 'Do not worry,' Calista said to her kindly. 'I hear they are often very courteous to ladies.'

'I am not worried,' said Blanche, her eyes flashing. But when the air was filled with the sound of gunshots, Blanche almost flew across the coach and into her mother's arms. 'Mama, if they kill me, I shall not have my Season.'

Calista wanted to laugh at that. Blanche always had her priorities right. One of Calista's biggest dreams was that Blanche would marry and go away so that she no longer had to put up with her insults, but she did not wish harm on her step-sister. Calista was no blushing violet when it came to dealing with Blanche, but the constant fight to defend herself left her exhausted at the end of most days. It was not in her nature to be unkind to anyone, yet there had been times when she was afraid she was becoming as bad as Blanche.

When the carriage door opened, Calista gave an involuntary scream but was determined to face the man down. If he shot her, then he would have to do so whilst looking her in the eyes.

'Do not be afraid,' a deep, resonant voice said. 'The highwayman has been captured.' Calista looked towards the door and was faced with a man unlike any she had ever seen. He was about thirty years old and dressed in the height of fashion, but without looking like one of the over-dressed dandies and rakes she read about in the gossip columns. He was tall and dark, clean- shaven, with flint-grey eyes and hawklike eyebrows. He looked directly at Calista and even if he had not told her the highwayman was under arrest, she would know she was safe with this man.

'I was not afraid,' said Blanche, before Calista could reply. 'It was my step-sister who screamed.'

Calista's lips turned up at the corners and she fought to suppress a smile.

'Well then you are a very brave lady indeed not to be afraid,' said the man with a hint of sarcasm in his voice. 'Please ladies, step out of the carriage. It is quite safe. I have a flask of brandy, and I think you could all benefit from a drink.' He reached out his hand to Calista, who was nearest to him.

One by one he helped them all out of the carriage. When Calista's legs touched the ground, she was perturbed to see that they shook beneath her. She looked around and saw another man standing some way off, holding on to the highwayman.

The man who had opened the carriage door spoke. 'Please, allow me to introduce myself. I am Colonel Windebank.' He naturally turned to Evelyn, as the eldest of the three women.

'We are very grateful for your help, Colonel Windebank.' Evelyn curtseyed, with Blanche and Calista following suit. 'I am Mrs. Haywood. This is my daughter, Miss Blanche Kirkham, and my step-daughter, Miss Calista Haywood. We are on our way to London for the Season.'

'Then do allow us to accompany you the rest of the way in case there is any more trouble.'

'Brook?' The man holding the prisoner spoke for the first time.

'What is it, Harry?'

'What are we to do with him?'

'Let him go, but keep his gun.'

'That's very good of you, Colonel Windebank, sir,' said the highwayman. He was not very old. No more than twenty-two or -three. The Colonel walked towards him.

'You're an idiot, Jimmy, but I know you've struggled to find work since the war ended. I'll write you a note to take to my estate, where you'll be given a job and a cottage. You can write to your wife and child and ask them to join you.'

'I don't deserve this, sir,' said Jimmy.

'No, you probably don't. Especially for terrorizing three women. But I've fought with you. I know you're a good man at heart. Go on, be off with you. If I find you've done something like this again, I shan't help you. Come on, Harry. We'll continue our journey.'

The man called Harry let Jimmy go and walked forward, bowing to the ladies, who curtseyed in return. He was a good-looking man in his late thirties. He stopped when he saw Mrs. Haywood. 'Evelyn? Evelyn Morehampton?'

Calista's eyes widened in surprise. It was rather a familiar address.

'Yes . . . Oh my goodness. It's Mr. Benedict, is it not? I have not seen you since I cannot remember when.' Yet when Evelyn spoke, Calista had the impression that she knew exactly when she had last seen Harry Benedict. Her delight seemed to be tinged with something else that Calista could not put a finger on. Fear? Surely not. The man seemed personable enough.

'More than twenty years ago.'

'It seems that no introductions are needed,' said the Colonel with a smile.

'I have not had the pleasure of meeting these two delightful young ladies,' said Mr. Benedict. Evelyn introduced Blanche and Calista.

'Miss Kirkham, Miss Haywood, I am very pleased to make your acquaintance. Your mother and I were good friends a long time ago, Miss Kirkham.'

'Really, how fascinating.' Blanche was not interested. She only had eyes for the Colonel, for which Calista could not blame her. He had shown himself to be not only brave, but also merciful. 'I am very eager to reach London, Colonel Windebank.'

'I thought,' said the Colonel, 'that we

might accompany the ladies, Harry. With your permission, Mrs. Haywood?' Evelyn bowed and thanked him. 'We will tie the horses to the back of the carriage and sit inside with them. It will surprise any other ruffians who wish to try their luck.'

A short time later they all sat in the carriage together, as they neared London.

'I cannot believe that we met again under such circumstances,' Mr. Benedict said to Evelyn. He had not taken his eyes from her since they got into the coach.

'It was certainly lucky that you happened along,' she replied.

'Are you on your way to London for the Season, Colonel?' asked Blanche.

'No, I was merely on my way to check on my home in London.'

'I am sure it is still there,' said Blanche, laughing a little bit too gaily.

'But sadly in very bad repair due to me being abroad for extended periods of time. This is why Mr. Benedict accompanies me. He is going to tell me how I may improve upon the house.'

'Of course, you were training to be an architect,' said Evelyn. 'I remember now.'

'Father was an architect too,' said Calista.

'My dear step-father, Bryan,' said Blanche, 'we all miss him dreadfully.' That was a surprise to Calista, but she clamped her lips shut.

'Haywood?' said the Colonel. 'Not Bryan Haywood?'

'Yes, that is correct,' said Calista. 'You knew my father?'

'I certainly knew of him. In fact . . . and please do not take offence, Harry . . . I had him in mind for some of the renovations, only to learn of his sad death.'

'No offence taken,' said Mr. Benedict with a smile.

'Please accept my condolences, Mrs. Haywood, Miss Haywood.' Calista noted that the Colonel did not include Blanche in his condolences. 'I was very taken by some of the buildings your father created in Derbyshire, Miss Haywood. Then sadly I had to settle for Harry.'

'Do not push your luck, Brook,' said Mr. Benedict. Calista could not help noticing how easy the two men were together. 'You did rather a lot of that during the war, when all we underlings could do was follow you.'

'You are wondering, are you not, Miss Haywood, how Mr. Benedict dares to be so familiar with a superior officer?' His eyes twinkled and his tone was self-deprecating. 'He and I spent a lot of time together during the war. One soon learns that it is rather dangerous to point one man out as the leader of the troop. Besides, Harry is a good and honest friend and we all need that.'

Blanche cut in, 'Then I shall always be honest with you, Colonel. And one day, perhaps I may be allowed to call you Brook.'

'Blanche!' her mother admonished her.

'And what of you, Miss Haywood?'

said the Colonel. 'Will you always be honest with me?'

'I would hope I am always honest, Colonel.'

'Wait until I tell everyone in London that we were rescued by a dashing Colonel,' said Blanche, clapping her hands together.

'I cannot take full credit for that,' said the Colonel. 'Harry was the one who saw you were in danger.' He turned once again to Calista. 'You look troubled, Miss Haywood.'

'I am only thinking that it is sad that the highwayman has suffered so much he turned to crime. Not that I condone his actions or have any reason to criticize yours, Colonel. It is just that I have heard that many soldiers are struggling since the end of the war.'

'Yes, the problem of the returning soldiers is something we hope to address in Parliament. But be aware that had we not caught him, in his desperation he might have harmed, even killed, you all. It has happened too often lately. At the very least he would have taken all your money and belongings. Then Miss Kirkham would not have her Season.' When his eyes twinkled again, Calista realized that he had heard everything that went on inside the coach before he opened the door.

'Where are you staying in London?' asked Mr. Benedict when they were nearing the outskirts.

'Lady Bedlington has agreed to let us stay with her, and she will introduce the girls to society,' said Evelyn.

'Goodness, is she still alive? I remember her chasing us off her land in Midchester when we stole some apples.'

'I am hoping she has forgotten,' said Evelyn. 'So please do not remind her.'

'You stole apples? Mama, really,' said Blanche, blushing. 'You shame me in front of the Colonel.'

'I assure you, Miss Kirkham,' said Colonel Windebank, 'I have stolen a few apples in my time. It is something all children do.'

'And soldiers too,' said Mr. Benedict

grimly. The Colonel looked at him and nodded just as grimly. Calista immediately understood that they too had gone through some very severe hardships during the war.

'I am sure I never did,' said Blanche. 'But if you say it is permissible, perhaps I shall try it.'

'I do not think it is as forgivable in an adult. At least not in peacetime. We certainly cannot run as fast. Have you ever stolen apples, Miss Haywood?'

'I'm sure she stole loads,' said Blanche. 'Her father was very poor.'

'And yet we did not have to steal to eat,' said Calista quietly. Then she smiled, mischievously. 'But I have climbed a few apple trees, Colonel.' She said it more to shock Blanche than anyone else.

'I am glad to hear it. To be surrounded by so much virtue can make a man feel inadequate.'

'Perhaps, Colonel, you will call upon us whilst you are in London,' said Blanche. 'I am sure Lady Bedlington would not mind.'

'Great Aunt Agatha would no doubt be delighted.'

'Great Aunt Agatha? I had not realized you and Lady Bedlington were related,' said Evelyn. Calista wondered why he had not mentioned it when Lady Bedlington's name was first mentioned.

'Yes, though I have not seen her for some time. Every time I see her she insists on trying to marry me off.'

'I am sure no one could force you to marry anyone, Colonel,' said Blanche.

It seemed to Calista that it was about the most honest thing Blanche had said so far, even if Blanche clearly had her own ideas about the Colonel's marital status. She was beautiful enough to entice him. Whether she would decide the Colonel was a little too far down the social ladder was another matter.

They reached Lady Bedlington's house in central London by early evening. Her Ladyship had gone out to dinner. The Colonel and Mr. Benedict said their goodbyes, leaving Evelyn and the two girls to settle in.

'I will call on you,' Mr. Benedict said to Evelyn. 'If you will permit it, that is.'

'I should like to see you again. Thank you again for your help, Colonel, Mr. Benedict.' Evelyn curtseyed, closely followed by the two girls.

'You are most welcome,' said the Colonel. 'I hope we shall see you again.' Calista glanced up at the Colonel, surprised to find he was looking at her. 'All of you.'

2

'Mama, you are not to see that man again. I forbid it.'

'Blanche, you are in no position to forbid me to do anything. Do remember that you are not yet twenty-one and I am still your mother.'

Calista gazed out of the window whilst her step-sister and Evelyn had yet another one of their rows. The square was coming to life as the tradespeople arrived with their wares and young ladies took a walk in the park that decorated the centre. She longed to be out there, and was indeed wearing her coat in readiness, but Blanche had much to say.

She had hoped that being in London would at least appease her step-sister, but Mr. Benedict's familiarity with Evelyn had infuriated her.

The previous evening had been quiet

enough. Even Blanche was not too silly as to behave badly in front of Lady Bedlington, whom she relied upon to introduce her to the correct society. She was also happy with the rooms they had been given, which overlooked a leafy London square. But when a message had arrived that morning from Mr. Benedict, asking if he may call upon Evelyn later that day, Blanche had waited until they were back up in their own rooms, getting ready to go out for a walk, before erupting.

'You will not marry yet another penniless architect,' said Blanche.

'Mr. Benedict is an old friend, Blanche. I have no intention of marrying him.'

'I am pleased to hear it. You can do better.'

Calista was aware that Blanche glanced at her as she said it, but was in no mood to argue. If Blanche did not appreciate their surroundings, Calista did. She gazed back at the square, praying for the argument to end so that she might make the most of the morning. It seemed to her that every day began with some disagreement. Blanche did not like her dress. Blanche did not like her breakfast. Blanche did not like Calista being involved in their entertainments. It was exhausting. Calista closed her eyes and let the faint breeze from the window cool her brow. It was pointless getting angry with Blanche, because one could never win the argument.

'I am rather too old to attract the attentions of a member of the aristocracy, dearest. But my friends are my own affair.'

'Father would not be very happy at how far down we have fallen,' said Blanche.

'Might I remind you, dearest, that your father was not a rich man and that all he did have was entailed away, leaving us penniless.'

'Father was part of the nobility. A distant relative of the Duke of Devonshire.'

'Hmm,' said Evelyn.

'Is that true?' asked Calista, when

Blanche had stormed out of the room.

Evelyn came and sat on the window seat next to her. 'Only by marriage and then very distantly. But Cedric rather liked to play up the connection. He used to tell Blanche that she would one day marry a Duke.'

'I wish you would not let her speak to you so unkindly,' said Calista.

'It upsets you to hear anyone being unkind, dear. I am sorry that our squabbles are spoiling your first full day in London. Sadly Blanche treats me as her father did, even though she does not know the reason.'

'What do you mean?' Calista looked at Evelyn sharply.

'Nothing.' Evelyn looked suddenly very sad. 'She is right. I cannot see Mr. Benedict again.'

'Why ever not? If you like him and he likes you.'

'For your sake, dearest.'

'Mine? I would not stop you if you wanted to marry again.'

'You do know, do you not, that your

father's estate is only available to me for my lifetime or until I marry again? Not that I am suggesting Mr. Benedict and I will ever marry. But if I did marry anyone, I may not be able to take care of you. I would hope I would meet someone who cares about you as I do, but husbands can be very strange about such things. Taking on my daughter is one thing, but taking on my step-daughter is not something I could guarantee.'

'I would not hold you back, Evelyn.'

'I know that. This is why you are so dear to me.' Evelyn kissed Calista's cheek. 'Sometimes I wish . . . Oh never mind. I am sorry that Blanche treats you so cruelly.'

'I can take care of myself.'

'I know you can. But I can also see what it costs you to have to stick up for yourself. When I first met you, you were a bright, cheerful little thing. Now I see sadness in your eyes, especially when Blanche and I argue.'

'I am just not used to it. Mama and Papa seldom argued. I suppose being an only child, I was also spared the problems of sibling rivalry. I just wish Blanche did not hate me so much. When you came to us, I was so happy that I had a sister at last and now . . . ' Calista's voice faded away. She did not really like criticizing Blanche to her step-mother.

When her widowed father had first announced his intention to marry the widow of an old school friend, Calista, who was fifteen at the time, had been delighted for him. She had known, of course, that he had started visiting Midchester a lot after he had attended Mr. Kirkham's funeral, but it was a year before he brought Evelyn and Blanche to their home. As Calista had told Evelyn, she had hoped she and Blanche would be proper sisters, but Blanche had hated Calista, hated her father, and hated their home. Blanche's own father, as Evelyn had pointed out, had filled Blanche's head full of her own importance.

Calista's mother and father had also

nurtured her in a way that gave her confidence, but they had not pretended that the family were anything other than they were: landed gentry, and on the lower end of the scale at that. Her father, who had a small annuity, had not earned much as an architect. Her mother had been ill for a very long time and he was reluctant to leave home, which was why most of his work was done in the Derbyshire area. By the time he was able to work again, he told Calista, 'Younger men are coming up now, dearest, with newer, fresher ideas. No one wants your old Papa.' She wished he could have known that Colonel Windebank had thought of him when looking for an architect. More than that, she wished he had lived long enough to be able to do it. He was very talented, regardless of what he said about his age.

Evelyn stroked her hair and said in a quiet voice, 'I understand, dearest. I love my daughter, but sometimes, may God forgive me, I do not like her very much. She frightens me sometimes. I believe that she will stop at nothing to get her own way and is willing to tread on anyone who gets in her path.'

Half an hour later, strolling out in the sunshine, even Blanche could not spoil Calista's enjoyment. They were going to Bond Street to order their new dresses, and whilst Calista would normally insist she did not care about finery, even she could not deny a sense of excitement at the thought of owning a fine new ball gown.

'Lady Bedlington said that Bond Street was built by a syndicate,' said Calista. 'It used to overlook open fields. Now it has many of the fine arts houses, including Sotheby's.'

'Fascinating,' said Blanche in her usual bored manner. 'But we are going to buy dresses, not antiques. Of course, when I am married to a rich man, I am sure I shall want to furnish my house accordingly, and then I'll worry about fine arts.'

'Do not give your heart to the first

person you meet,' said Evelyn. 'You have not appeared in society yet. You may fall in love with someone without a title, dearest.'

'I do not think so. Lady Bedlington told me that Colonel Windebank is very rich. Probably one of the richest men in England. I cannot find a better catch.'

'Perhaps you should let him be the one to catch you,' Evelyn suggested. 'Men do not approve of women who pursue them. It is not the way a lady should behave.'

'Well of course, Mama, what do you take me for? However, I noticed that he could not keep his eyes off me in the carriage yesterday. I believe a proposal will be forthcoming.'

Sometimes Calista wished she had Blanche's confidence. Evelyn was quite right about her daughter. She would have what she wanted and not care who she stepped upon to get it. Given that young ladies of their time were not allowed to earn money any other way, perhaps Blanche was more realistic than most. Calista longed to marry someone who loved her, and whom she loved in return. Sadly the cold, hard truth was if she did not find a husband, if Evelyn did marry again, she would be left penniless and alone in the world. That would inevitably happen when Evelyn died, even though she had many years left yet.

Suddenly the idea of the new dresses seemed less exciting, because they could be seen as a means of luring a man into marriage and Calista did not wish to do that. If Evelyn remarried, she would find some way to support herself. She was good at needlework, so she could make dresses for the local gentry who were not as well off and could not afford London fashion prices.

Not one to stay glum for long, Calista soon became caught up in the excitement of ordering new clothes. Even Blanche could not spoil it with her barbed comments. 'I do not think that colour suits you,' Blanche said more than once. 'You should wear grey to suit your personality.'

'Blanche . . . ' Evelyn cut in mildly. 'You look very pretty, Calista. That shade of blue suits your eyes.' Then, as if she thought she was being unkind to her daughter, 'You look magnificent, Blanche. I am sure you will break lots of hearts before the Season is over.' Blanche did indeed look very beautiful in a dress of dark red, which contrasted well with her dark hair and eyes.

'The first heart I shall break will be the Colonel's,' Blanche said, loftily. 'He is a very handsome man, and I hear very rich, but whilst we were walking it occurred to me that he does not have a title. However, I shall find him interesting to practise upon and it will make other, more important men jealous when they see him making love to me.'

'I am sure it will, dearest.'

With their purchases completed, they returned to Lady Bedlington's house, only to find she had visitors. As they approached the drawing room, they heard Her Ladyship say, 'It is most irregular, Brook.'

'I realize that, Aunt Agatha,' said the Colonel, 'but it is how I wish things to be for now.'

'Ah,' Mr. Benedict cut in, with what seemed to be a warning note in his voice. 'I believe the ladies have returned.'

'I have pleasing news,' said Lady Bedlington, after the greetings were completed and everyone was seated. 'My nephew and his friend, Mr. Benedict, will be staying with us for a few days.' Lady Bedlington was an elderly woman of indeterminate age. She was known for her sharp tongue, but could also be very charming. Calista had liked her immediately, although their meeting the previous evening had been somewhat brief.

'I hope we will not intrude upon you,' said the Colonel.

'Not at all,' said Evelyn. 'It is, of course, Her Ladyship's business whom she invites, but we are all very pleased to see you again.'

'Yes, I have been hearing about your

adventures,' said Lady Bedlington. 'Really, what is this world coming to when three ladies of good standing are assaulted in such a way? They should hang them all.' Calista could not be certain, but she had the distinct idea that Her Ladyship was being deliberately provocative rather than saying what she really believed.

'I fear you will disturb Miss Haywood by saying so,' said the Colonel. 'She is very sorry for the highwaymen.'

Calista blushed, feeling that he was teasing her. 'I only feel, as I told you, Colonel, that a man must be very desperate to turn to crime.'

'I concede that, Miss Haywood. I did not mean to cause offence.'

'You are a young woman with a good heart, Miss Haywood,' said Lady Bedlington, 'and I cannot censure you for that.'

'I too think it is tragic,' said Blanche. 'I imagine the poor man lives in a hovel, without doors or windows.'

'I rather think he would have trouble

leaving the hovel if there were no door,' said Mr. Benedict. When he saw the flash of anger in Blanche's eyes, he added hastily, 'Forgive me, Miss Kirkham, I only talk in jest.'

'I am sure you are thought very amusing amongst your own kind,' said Blanche.

'Blanche,' Evelyn hissed under her breath.

'My father, Mr. Kirkham, was part of the nobility,' Blanche said to Lady Bedlington, ignoring her mother.

'Kirkham? Kirkham?' Lady Bedlington frowned. 'I do not believe I am familiar with the Kirkhams. I know your mother, of course, as one of the Morehamptons. A very fine old family from Midchester. Do you remember them, Brook?'

'Yes, indeed, though I had not had the pleasure of meeting Mrs. Kirkham until yesterday.'

'But you had, Mr. Benedict, I am sure. In fact,' Lady Bedlington smiled and it was very charming, 'I remember you both stealing my apples. Scrumping, they call it in Midchester.'

'I am most embarrassed that my mother did such a thing,' said Blanche.

'Do not be, child. She was young, and full of high spirits. You may not believe it, but I was young once myself.'

'You are young now, My Lady,' said Blanche. 'Why, I do not believe you can be a day over seventy.'

'I am sixty-five,' said Lady Bedlington. But as she said it, she winked at her great nephew. Calista lowered her head so that her smile was not too obvious. 'And you, child,' Lady Bedlington said, addressing Calista, 'my great nephew tells me that your father was an architect.'

'That is correct, My Lady.'

'I knew the Haywoods of course, as a young lady. Everyone did. A most talented family. I believe your late uncle was a painter was he not and that his portrait of the King is very well thought of.'

'I believe so, My Lady.'

'The Haywoods were related to

nobility, did you know that, Brook?'

'No, Aunt Agatha, I did not.'

'Yes. If I am correct in thinking so, Miss Haywood's grandmother was the youngest child of Lord Norton. Their family is very artistic. Are you artistic, Miss Haywood?'

Blanche, clearly deciding Calista had had enough attention said, 'I am told, though it is not for me to say, that I play the pianoforte to perfection. Perhaps I could play for you one night.'

'I was speaking of Miss Haywood. Are you as artistic as the rest of your family, child?'

'I paint a little,' said Calista. 'And I write poetry. I . . . ' She paused, afraid that what she said next would be considered shocking.

'Yes, do go on.'

'I like to design buildings, though I do not have my father's talent.'

'It is hardly a pursuit for a lady,' said Blanche. 'Do you not think, Lady Bedlington?'

'The Countess of Shrewsbury helped

to design Chatsworth House and Hardwick Hall,' said Calista, hotly.

'Bess of Hardwick,' said Lady Bedlington. 'Yes, she was a rather formidable, but very talented, woman. Chatsworth is a masterpiece. Not that I am quite so old that I knew her.' Her Ladyship's eyes twinkled in Blanche's direction, but Blanche seemed not to notice.

'Calista also redesigned some of our old dresses,' said Evelyn. 'She copied styles from the latest magazines to do so. I do not think anyone would notice they are not brand new.'

'They will now you have said, Mama,' Blanche muttered.

'That is very sensible,' said Lady Bedlington. 'Women spend far too much on clothes. I still have dresses that I purchased twenty years ago. My maid does her best to redesign them but perhaps you might take a look at them whilst you are here, Miss Haywood.'

'I would be glad to be of any assistance,' said Calista.

'Of course,' said Blanche, 'I was only

saying this morning, 'Mama, you must not spend so much on clothes. It is a waste of money.' She would not listen and insisted I had all the accessories I needed.'

Calista clamped her lips shut, remembering that particular tantrum well. Blanche had attracted the attention of everyone in the shop.

'Well . . . ' said the Colonel, standing up. 'Whilst this talk of fashion is all very fascinating, Mr. Benedict and I must arrange to have our luggage brought over.'

'We forgot you were there, dear,' said Lady Bedlington, smiling benignly.

The Colonel bowed. 'Perhaps, Miss Haywood, you would permit me to see some of your designs one day. Of buildings, that is, not dresses.'

'I fear I may well be out of a job soon,' said Mr. Benedict, with a kind smile in Calista's direction. 'Especially if you do have your father's talent.'

'As dearest Calista has told you in her customary modest way,' said Blanche, 'she is not very good.'

'I hope she will allow us to be the judge of her talent,' said the Colonel. 'As we will be when you play the pianoforte for us, Miss Kirkham.'

Calista was not sure, but she suspected there might have been an insult lurking in the Colonel's words.

'I shall very much look forward to playing for you,' said Blanche, looking up at him through lowered lashes.

3

Calista sat in the garden and listened. For once all she could hear was the sound of birds singing. Blanche had been invited to visit two young sisters she had met at dinner the night before, and it was made clear that Calista was not invited. Evelyn had left with Blanche, apologizing to Calista as she did so.

She did not mind. The sisters had been vacuous in the extreme and she was more than happy to take a break from her step-sister. The previous afternoon had been dominated by another tantrum about Calista monopolizing Lady Bedlington.

'I can hardly ignore her when she addresses me directly,' said Calista.

'Oh don't play the innocent, Calista. You were pushing yourself forward. What did you mean saying that you liked to design buildings? I suppose that was to get the Colonel's attention. Do you really wonder at why he has asked to stay with his aunt? He wishes to be close to me. It is perfect, as if my plan were meant to be.'

Calista closed her eyes. She would not think about the argument. Not whilst she had the chance to be alone with her own thoughts.

'I hope I am not interrupting you, Miss Haywood.'

Her eyes opened, and immediately looked up into the Colonel's grey eyes. 'Of course not, Colonel. I was just taking the air.'

'And enjoying the peace and quiet?'

'Yes. It is not often I have time alone.'

'I can leave.' He smiled wryly.

'I did not mean that . . . '

'No, I understand what you mean. Your step-sister is . . . vigorous.'

Calista laughed. 'That is one way to describe her.'

'And very cruel to you.'

'I am sure she does not mean half of what she says.' Why Calista felt the need to defend Blanche, she did not know. She supposed family was family. Plus, it was not in her nature to criticize people behind their backs. If she had something to say to Blanche, she said it to her face, as exhausting as that was at times.

'I wondered if you would like to come and see my house, so that I can share my plans with you so far.'

'I am afraid my step-mother is out with Blanche,' said Calista. As much as she would have liked to go with him, it would not be proper for her to go out with him alone.

'I have already considered that. My aunt has agreed to accompany us, so you will be chaperoned. She has asked Cook to prepare us a luncheon.'

'I . . . '

'Are you not curious about my plans?'

'Yes, yes, I am. And I should like very much to see your house and hear about them. Thank you.'

An hour later, they stood in the hall of a crumbling mansion somewhere in the centre of London. 'As you can see, it is great need of renovation, hence my presuming on your hospitality, Aunt Agatha.'

'Yes, your uncle was most neglectful,' said Lady Bedlington. She exchanged a glance with the Colonel.

'Harry has been working on the plans. I hope to have several bathrooms installed, along with plumbing.'

'It is a beautiful old building, even without renovation,' said Calista. 'I agree it is need of updating, but I hope you will not change too much. The Corinthian columns in this hall are very beautiful.' There were four columns of amber marble on each side of the hall, set about six feet apart and leading to the sweeping staircase.

'I promise I shall not make changes for the sake of change, Miss Haywood. Though I would rather like to open up the drawing room a little more, by combining it with a small sitting room. It is upstairs. Perhaps you will let me show you.'

'You both may go, Brook,' said Lady Bedlington. 'I will seek solace in the study with a glass of sherry. I find stairs too much of a trial nowadays.'

As far as Calista recalled, Lady Bedlington did not appear to have any problems with the stairs in her own home.

The Colonel gestured for Calista to go ahead of him up the stairs. 'Unfortunately much of the wood on the banister is rotted,' he explained. 'So I will replace that as soon as possible. Do be careful there.'

As he spoke, the banister under Calista's hand crumbled, causing her to lose her balance slightly. She felt his hands on her waist as he caught her and helped her to stay upright. Her back rested against his muscular chest. 'I apologise, Miss Haywood, I should have warned you sooner.'

'I am well now,' she said, realizing that he still held her. He moved his hands away, yet she could still feel the impression of them upon her waist and the warmth of his body against hers. She continued to the top of the stairs, more gingerly this time. She hoped he could not hear her ragged breath.

'How long have you owned this house?' she asked when she reached the top. She turned around to face him, trying to keep her conversation calm even though she felt anything but.

'Windebank House has been in my mother's family for many years,' he replied. 'But I did not come here until recently, when my uncle died and it was left to me. He lived mostly in the country, and as a bachelor, when he was in London he stayed at his club rather than here. It was once a great family home and I hope to make it that again.'

'It already has strong foundations,' said Calista, smiling. 'I am sure it will be wonderful once you have finished. But a house needs people to be a home.'

'Then we are in accordance. That is what I believe. Come, the drawing room is this way.'

He took her to a room to the left of the staircase and with large sash windows overlooking the square. He threw open the shutters to reveal a room that had once been grand but which, like many of the others in the house, had fallen into disrepair. Dust sheets covered the furniture, and the fireplace was full of ashes. She wondered when the house had last had servants. She guessed that the Colonel's uncle had not wanted to pay them if he never stayed there.

'What a wonderful room,' she said. The Colonel opened a door at the far end, and said, 'This is the sitting room I wish to combine with this one.'

'I hope you do not mind me saying,' said Calista, 'but I think this would make a wonderful library. The space is similar to that at Blenheim Palace. Papa took me there when I was a child, and I remember the library. I believe it is over one hundred and eighty feet in length. If you could combine all the rooms on this side of the house . . . ' She stopped.

'I apologise, Colonel. I am speaking out of turn. It will also make a very charming drawing room.'

'Yes, I have seen Blenheim Palace. Vanburgh was a fine architect.' The Colonel was looking at her in a way that unnerved her. 'I do not think I have nearly enough books to fill such a library, but it sounds very grand.'

'And perhaps not fitting for a family home.'

The Colonel folded his arms and leaned against the wall next to the window. 'Tell me about yourself, Miss Haywood.'

'What do you wish to know?' Calista continued to walk around the room, looking at the old wallpaper and the architecture, feeling shy about the way the Colonel's grey eyes pierced into her. 'My father, as you know, was an architect. He died two years ago. Mama was also an artist. She never showed her work, of course. She died when I was ten. Papa married again when I was fifteen. Evelyn . . . Mrs. Haywood . . . has been every bit a mother to me. She too is a talented artist, though she is too modest to say so . . . I am sorry, Colonel — have I said something wrong?' Calista had stopped talking long enough to notice that he was frowning.

'No, nothing wrong at all. Apart from the fact that I have asked you about you and all you have talked about is your father, mother and step-father.'

'I suppose I am unused to talking about myself.'

'Yes, Blanche does seem to over-shadow everyone else.' His perception only served to unnerve Calista all the more. 'Now, please, tell me about you. I know that you paint . . . a little. And write poetry . . . a little. You clearly have an eye for architecture. What else should I know about you?'

'I am afraid you would find me very boring, Colonel. I like to walk through the woods in spring when the bluebells are in bloom. I like to make mince pies at Christmas. Unfortunately I also like to eat them, which means that every

January I have to let all my dresses out. I like to read the reports from Parliament, though no doubt that is shocking for a young lady.'

'Surprising, but not shocking.'

'You think that women are incapable of understanding politics?'

'No, I know of women who are more than capable. But young ladies are a different matter. Most of those I'm forced to spend time with would prefer to be told how beautiful they are.'

'I can assure you that you need not waste time on that with me.' Calista smiled.

'And yet you are very beautiful.'

'Now you have disappointed me,' said Calista, feeling flustered and trying to make a jest of his words. 'Only a few minutes ago you spoke to me as an equal. Now you are treating me as you treat all other women.'

'I promise you I will never do that, Calista. But we had vowed to always be honest with each other, had we not?' His use of her first name flustered her all the more.

'I think I promised to be honest with you, Colonel. I do not recall you making such a promise to me.' It seemed to Calista that the air around them crackled with electricity.

'Then it was very remiss of me. I promise now that I will always be honest with you. And that includes my remark about your beauty.'

'I think that perhaps we should return to Lady Bedlington. She will wonder where we are.'

'And there you go again. Turning the conversation to others when I wish to discuss you.'

'I have told you, Colonel, I am not used to it.'

'Very well, Miss Haywood, but I do intend to learn everything there is to know about you.'

'Then there will be nothing left to discover and you will be bored.'

'With you? I doubt that very much.'

Calista left the room without answering him. Is this what happened when a man made love to a woman? Despite

Blanche's insistence that Calista monopolized the young men in Derbyshire, she had not had much experience of being wooed. She could only suppose the Colonel was being polite. Or perhaps he was flirting with her because he was bored and had nothing better to do. She imagined that the women he preferred to spend time with were more worldly-wise and sophisticated. She had heard that the ladies who graced the London Season were called the *Incomparables*. She was hardly that.

Or perhaps he only paid her attention because Blanche was not there. He said that Blanche overshadowed everyone else. Because Calista did not much like her step-sister, she had chosen to see it as a negative comment. Perhaps the Colonel meant it in a more positive way. She hoped not, because she now knew that Blanche only intended to use him to make other men jealous. Insisting to herself that it was the only reason she did not want the Colonel to like Blanche, she carried on downstairs to go in search of Lady Bedlington.

They ate their luncheon in a small dining room at the back of the house. 'I am afraid,' said the Colonel, 'that the main dining room is not fit for company as yet.'

'It is a good job I agreed to put you up, Brook,' said Lady Bedlington. 'Where on earth were you planning to sleep?'

'Harry and I have slept in worse places. But we were going to stay at the club. When I realized you were in town, Aunt Agatha, I knew you would give us shelter.'

'Is that the only reason you decided to stay in my house?' Lady Bedlington's eyes twinkled, and for the first time, Calista noticed how much alike Great Aunt and Great Nephew were. Lady Bedlington was handsome in the way a man was rather than a lady, and she had the same grey eyes.

'Of course.'

'So, Miss Haywood,' said Lady Bedlington. 'What would you do to my great nephew's house? Apart from knocking it all down and starting from scratch, which I feel may be a better idea. His uncle never did take care of this house.'

'I think it is a wonderful house,' said Calista. 'Though I fear I may have suggested a rather expensive renovation upstairs. A library to rival that in Blenheim Palace.'

'Oh that caused a scandal. Not the library particularly, but the palace. You are aware perhaps that the first Duke of Marlborough, John Churchill, was given the house by Queen Anne, who was great friends with his wife, Sarah Churchill. Then they had a falling out and Her Majesty refused to continue paying for the building project. The Churchills had to go into exile.'

'Ah, so that was a ploy by Miss Haywood to force me out of the country,' said the Colonel.

'You have been out of the country too often and too long,' said Lady Bedlington. Then, as if something else had occurred to her, she said, 'You know that the Duke of Midchester is in town and that he has a new favourite, do you not?'

'Really?' For reasons Calista could not fathom, the Colonel seemed to be on his guard.

'Yes, young Ronald Purbeck. A distant cousin, I believe. They say that His Grace will name Purbeck as his heir.'

'He may do as he wishes with his titles and lands,' said the Colonel. His lips set in a thin line.

'Oh but Brook . . . ' Lady Bedlington stopped and glanced at Calista. 'I am sure Miss Haywood will soon be bored if we discuss people she does not know.'

'Please do not mind me,' said Calista. 'I realize you have not seen each other for a while.'

'No, we must not exclude you,' said the Colonel.

'I should like, if you do not mind, Lady Bedlington, to know more of the squabble between the Churchills and Queen Anne. If that is not presumptuous of me.'

The rest of the luncheon was spent in lively conversation about the trials and tribulations of the first Duke and Duchess of Marlborough and the building of Blenheim Palace. After lunch, the Colonel showed Calista around the rest of the house, outlining his plans for renovation, but always asking her opinion. That too led to lively discussions. She could not remember when she had last enjoyed a day so much. Most of her happy moments were stolen, when she was able to slip out of Haywood Manor and go walking alone. In winter, when it was impossible to go outside, days spent in Blanche's company became unbearable, despite Evelyn's attempts to pour oil on troubled waters.

'Thank you for showing me your house,' she said to the Colonel when they travelled back to Lady Bedlington's home. 'I hope I will be able to see it when it is completed.'

'You will be amongst my first guests,' he promised.

Blanche and Evelyn had returned

home by the time they reached Lady Bedlington's. They were also accompanied by a young dandy of about twenty. He was handsome in what Calista thought was a rather bland way, and dressed in the height of fashion.

'Mr. Purbeck,' said Lady Bedlington. 'We were just discussing you.'

Mr. Purbeck bowed. 'I hope in good terms, Lady Bedlington.'

Lady Bedlington did not reply to that. Instead she made the introductions. 'You know my nephew, Colonel Brook Windebank, of course.'

'I have heard of your exploits on the battlefield, Colonel,' said Mr. Purbeck. Calista was not sure if she imagined it, but Mr. Purbeck did not seem to like the Colonel. 'How sorry I was that the war ended before I could do my bit.'

'I am sure the war's loss is society's gain,' said Blanche, fluttering her eyelashes at Mr. Purbeck.

'No doubt,' said the Colonel, with a wry smile.

'And this,' said Lady Bedlington, 'is

Miss Haywood.'

'Charmed, Miss Haywood, I am sure. I have been hearing all about you from your charming sister.' Calista did not like to imagine what Blanche had said to Mr. Purbeck, but she took the compliment at face value, curtseying to him.

'We met Mr. Purbeck this morning,' said Blanche, when they were all seated. 'He is in London with his cousin, the Duke of Midchester. The Duke has made a great favourite of Mr. Purbeck.'

'I do not like to boast,' said Mr. Purbeck, 'but His Grace finds me indispensible.' All the time he spoke, his eyes were on the Colonel.

'And yet he is managing without you at the moment,' said Lady Bedlington.

'What? Oh yes.' Mr. Purbeck laughed awkwardly. 'I have heard that you like to tease, Your Ladyship. He would approve, I am sure, of me making sure two ladies returned home safe.'

'Yes, it must have been treacherous travelling all the way from the next street,' said the Colonel.

'Unlike you, Colonel, I do not have the benefit of being able to save them from highwaymen.'

'I am sure you should be very brave if you did,' said Blanche. 'But the highwayman was not that much of a threat I am sure.'

Calista, Evelyn and the Colonel exchanged glances, each suppressing a grin.

'I wish to talk of other things,' said Blanche. 'Mr. Purbeck, via the Duke of Midchester, has secured us an invitation to Almacks for the Wednesday ball. Sadly only Mama and I may attend, Calista, as it would have been rude to ask the Duke for another invitation when he was so generous. I am not even sure you would benefit from the visit.'

Almacks was the most prestigious club in London. Unlike most clubs, it allowed both sexes. The female patronesses of the club ruled it with a rod of iron, and the people who were allowed to enter its hallowed halls were strictly regulated. The patronesses also had the power to refuse entry, and met every Monday night to decide who had committed a serious enough social faux pas to be excluded.

'I am sure,' said the Colonel, in a cold voice, 'that my Great Aunt has enough influence of her own to secure Miss Haywood an invitation. If she does not, then I do.'

'Oh no, please, do not bother on my account,' said Calista, her cheeks reddening.

'Brook is right,' said Lady Bedlington. 'I will ensure Miss Haywood goes to the ball.'

4

'I must take my leave,' said Mr. Purbeck, standing up. 'I shall look forward to seeing you all on Wednesday night. If I can bear to keep away.' He looked at Blanche as he spoke.

'Thank goodness he has gone,' said Lady Bedlington.

'You do not like him?' said Blanche.

'No, I do not like him. He is a popinjay and a sycophant.'

'But he is the Duke of Midchester's favourite,' said Blanche. 'He told us all about the quarrel the duke had with his son. Do you know that the son challenged his own father to a duel? It caused such a scandal and his son had to leave the country. After that, the duke cut his son out of the inheritance. Now, it is certain that Mr. Purbeck will be named his successor. He is so handsome, is he not?'

'I think I have made my feelings plain,' said Lady Bedlington.

'With all due respect, Your Ladyship, I think you are being unkind.'

'With all due respect, Miss Kirkham, I have reached an age when I can say what I wish. Mr. Purbeck seeks to deny the rightful heir to the Duchy of Midchester. I think you will find, despite your dreams and fantasies, that society has different ideas and that such a thing will not be so easy. All the rightful heir has to do is claim his inheritance and all Mr. Purbeck's plans are as dust.'

'Mr. Purbeck says that the duke's heir said he did not want to bear his father's name and title. He told his father he would rather starve in a garret than to do so. How can a son say such a thing to his father?'

'Perhaps,' said the Colonel, 'he had good reason.'

Calista looked at the Colonel and an idea began to form. Purbeck had been cold towards him. Lady Bedlington had made a point earlier of indicating Purbeck's interest in the title, but the Colonel had insisted that the duke may dispense of his lands and titles as he wished.

'Mr. Purbeck says that the duke's son is a dreadful man. Proud and stubborn.'

'Blanche,' said Evelyn in her quiet way, 'I do not think that it is correct for you to criticize a man you have never met.'

'And one to whom I'm related,' said Lady Bedlington.

'You're related . . . ' Blanche's face turned ashen. 'I had no idea. I mean . . . '

For Calista that gave her the proof she needed that the Colonel was the Duke's son. She realized his eyes were piercing into her, as if he followed her train of thought.

'Miss Haywood,' he said, when the other ladies were leaving the room to go up and change for dinner. 'Could I speak to you alone for a moment?'

Lady Bedlington glanced back and

smiled. 'You are allowed five minutes with her, Brook. Any more than that and I will barge in on you.'

Her Ladyship herded the others out of the room and shut the door.

'What is it, Colonel?'

'I suspect you have guessed my secret.'

'You are the duke's son?'

'Yes, but I would be grateful if you could keep that to yourself and do not even tell your step-mother and step-sister.'

'But surely others know. I think Mr. Purbeck does. He seemed to look at you strangely.'

'No, Purbeck has other reasons to dislike me. I was once romantically attached to his elder sister. Unfortunately I found out that she had already made a promise of marriage to another man. She told her family that I abandoned her, and I did not dispute the fact. If it salvaged her pride to think so, I was not about to deny her that small victory.'

'What I mean is that surely others know who you are anyway?'

'Great Aunt Agatha does, of course. But I took my mother's family name as soon as I was old enough. People know that my father has a son, but they do not know my birth name, and he has never acknowledged me publicly. I have seen my father twice in my life. Once when I was a baby, which naturally I do not remember. Apparently he came to see me at our relative's house, took one look at me and walked away. And once again when I called him out.'

'Would it be rude of me to ask why you did that?'

'My father may be a gentleman by birth but he is not a gentleman by deed. My late mother was sixteen when they married. It was arranged by the families so there were no illusions about it being a love match. However, from the very beginning my father treated her abominably, both physically and mentally. He was violent, and he paraded his mistresses in front of her in her own home. When she was seventeen years old and expecting me, she fled my father's house and went back to her family, fearing for her life after my father had flown into a drunken rage, egged on by his current mistress.' The Colonel's eyes became dark and brooding, as if the pain of thinking of his mother's suffering were too much for him.

'They protected her, of course, but she never spoke out against my father publicly. You are aware, I am sure, of the double standards that exist in society, Miss Haywood. A man, especially a nobleman, may behave as he pleases, but his wife must always be above reproach and is expected to put up with ill treatment in silence. She has no recourse in a court of law, and my father would not divorce her.'

The Colonel's eyes became sad. 'My mother died when I was five years old, but her family, perhaps mindful of the way she was treated, refused to let me return to my father for fear he may treat me just as badly. As it stands, they paid me a very great favour in doing so. I did go to my father when I was twenty-one, hoping to find him changed. It was a foolish notion.' He fell silent for a while, as if he was seeing the scene in his mind's eye. Calista, transfixed by the tragic story he told, said nothing. 'I suppose I thought that as he had come to see me when I was born, he had some interest in me. He denounced me on the spot. He said that my mother was a . . . ' He drew in his breath sharply. 'I shall not share that word with you. I will only assure you that my mother was everything that was good and pure in this world. That is not a son's delusion. That is the opinion of everyone who knew her.

My father denied that I was his son. I was furious. Not for me, but for the insult he paid my dear, gentle mother. So I challenged him to a duel. It was illegal to do so, and still is, but I felt that I owed it to my mother, who had been so badly treated, to protect her good name. I was a better shot than my father, but still I only winged him, simply to make my point. That was when he disowned me completely, saying that if I ever tried for the dukedom he would leave word with his lawyers that I was not his true heir. He claimed he had proof that my mother deceived him.'

'But that is not true.' Calista felt a lump in her throat. Having been loved and protected by both her parents, and then by Evelyn, she could hardly comprehend a father treating his wife and son so badly.

The Colonel smiled sadly. 'No, I am sure it is not. From the time she married till she left at seventeen, my mother was seldom in anyone's company but my father's. He made sure of that, so that his cruelty would not be discovered. But I would still not have her name sullied. Mud, as you know, Miss Haywood, sticks. I do not mind for myself. I have made my own fortune, and distinguished myself as a soldier. If I were thrown out of society because that society believed me to be illegitimate, I would survive. The hypocrisy that exists is astounding. The only commandment of the nobility is 'thou shalt not be found out'. I do not care if my father does disown me publicly as well as privately. But I will not stand by and let anyone cast aspersions on my mother's character. Not after all she suffered at his hands.'

'I am so sorry for both your suffering,' said Calista, as a tear slipped from her eye. She had an image of an eager young man, hoping that his father would accept him, despite everything. It must have hurt the Colonel far more than he pretended.

'I cannot say I suffered. My mother made sure of that by taking me to a safe haven where I was loved and nurtured.'

'It must have hurt deeply when your father disowned you.'

'Do not imbue me with a sensitivity I do not have, Miss Haywood. I can honestly say I hate my father, and am just as happy to disown him.' Despite his words, Calista believed he was telling a lie. She could not blame him. It was no doubt a way of protecting himself against the pain of his father's behaviour.

'I believe your five minutes are up,' said Lady Bedlington from the door. She smiled kindly at Calista, who curtseyed and went to leave the room. As Calista turned into the corridor, out of the corner of her eye she saw Lady Bedlington move across the room and put her hand on the Colonel's arm in a touching gesture, murmuring something in sympathetic tones that Calista did not quite hear.

Calista only wished that she had the courage to touch him in the same way. She would have done anything to take away his pain.

'What on earth did the Colonel want with you?' said Blanche when Calista arrived at their sitting room.

'He is renovating his house and asked my opinion on some things,' said Calista. She wished she did not have to deal with Blanche of all people. She felt moved by the Colonel's story and wanted to be alone to think about it. To think about him.

'Your opinion? Oh well, I am sure that is his way of trying to include you. Just like his insistence you go to Almacks. I think he feels sorry for you. Do not think he will marry you, Calista. You are far too unimportant for a man like the Colonel.'

'Blanche,' said Calista, her temper rising. 'Do you ever get tired of the sound of your own voice?' She brushed past Evelyn, ignoring the fact that her step-mother reached out for her, and went into her room, slamming the door after her.

She heard Blanche's muffled tones through the door. 'Mama, how could you let her speak to me in such a way? And me about to become a duchess.'

Calista lay on her bed in the darkened room, thinking of all she had been told. She realized how lucky she had been, to be raised first by two parents who loved each other dearly, with a gentle father and loving mother, and then to have Evelyn as a step-mother. Admittedly Blanche could be a problem, but even she did not behave violently towards Calista.

After half an hour, the door opened a little. 'Calista . . . ' It was Evelyn. 'May I come in, dearest?'

'Yes, of course.'

Evelyn shut the door and came to sit on the edge of Calista's bed. 'Blanche's words have hurt more than ever, have they not?'

'No, I do not care what Blanche says.'

Evelyn stroked Calista's arm. 'Oh I think you did then. I have known you to defend yourself to her, but never to give way to temper.'

'I am sorry.'

'You do not have to apologise to me, child. Nor to Blanche for that matter. She goes too far and it is good for her to be told when she is wrong. You like the Colonel, do you not?'

'Of course. He is a very fine gentle-man.'

'No, I mean you like him as a man. I was young once. I know that look in your eyes. But something else has upset you. Why did he wish to speak to you? Has he said something offensive to you?'

'Oh no, he would never do such a thing, Evelyn. I am afraid I am sworn to secrecy. I cannot tell you.'

'Very well, I will respect that. You are a good girl, Calista. I am sure he likes you too.'

'Blanche is right, I am sure. He just feels sorry for me and wishes to be kind. Not that I expect him to want to marry me. Unlike Blanche, I do not see every man I meet as a potential husband.'

'No, I think that when you fall in love, it will be once only and it will be the love of a lifetime.' Evelyn smiled.

'Is that how you felt about Blanche's father? When you married him, I mean.'

'No. Not really. We were fond of each other at first, but . . . I am afraid I have my secrets too, child. Some that are too painful to share and some that might explode and . . . '

'What?' Calista sat up. 'What is it, Evelyn? You may trust me with anything, I hope you know that.'

'Yes, I know, dear, but I fear from the look in your eyes that you are the keeper of enough secrets at the moment. When Blanche is safely married and nothing can be undone . . . then I may tell you. I can only hope that you will not think unkindly of me.'

'I am sorry if you have known pain,' said Calista, taking Evelyn's hand in hers. 'I would do anything to spare you from it.'

A tear formed in Evelyn's eye and rolled down her cheek. 'You are a dear girl and I love you as my own. We will find happiness, you and I, Calista. I know it.'

'But first we have to get Blanche married off,' Calista said impishly. 'I am sure there will be any number of Dukes in Almacks. Or Earls or Marquises. Perhaps now we are no longer at war with France, we could marry her off to a nice French diplomat and then she will go and live abroad.'

'You should not make me laugh at such things,' said Evelyn, giggling. 'Blanche is my daughter after all.'

'I am sorry,' said Calista, becoming serious.

'No, darling, do not be.' Evelyn squeezed her hand. 'I love your humour and Blanche does rather deserve it at times. Maybe we could even find a Russian diplomat. That is even further away.'

'Knowing Blanche she will be running Russia within six months. She will certainly give the Tsar a run for his money.'

'You are a wicked girl and I am not listening anymore.' Evelyn paused before bursting out laughing again. 'I gather Siberia is an interesting place to live.'

The bedroom door burst open. 'What on earth are you two laughing about? You're disturbing my sleep! I must look beautiful for tonight.'

'You always look beautiful, Blanche,'

said Calista, determined to be kind to Blanche to make up for her recent cattiness.

'What do you want, Calista?' Blanche's dark eyes narrowed.

'Nothing.'

'You must want something. You are never kind to me.'

'I have always tried to be, Blanche.'

'Then you should try harder.' Blanche left, slamming the door.

'Oh dear,' said Evelyn, 'the poor Tsar.'

Calista fell back on the bed, laughing hysterically.

5

Almacks was packed to the brim with nobility of all kinds, along with the young women taking their first official steps into society. Both Blanche and Calista were presented to the patronesses, who looked upon them both with favour.

'Do you enjoy visiting Almacks?' Calista asked Lady Bedlington as they made their way to the ballroom. Blanche had spied Mr. Purbeck across the room and made a rather undignified beeline for him, closely followed by her embarrassed mother.

'Not very much, child. It is grand enough but the patronesses insist no alcohol is served on the premises. Only lemonade. In my experience one cannot face the majority of the nobility without a strong drink to hand.'

Calista laughed. 'I think I am already

drunk on the atmosphere.' It was certainly heady. Everyone was dressed in their finery, and Calista could not remember when she had seen more beautiful gowns and in every conceivable colour. The simple pale blue gown she wore seemed drab by comparison. Her fair hair had been set up in the French style, and was adorned with a wide blue ribbon to match her dress. She instinctively put her hand to her hair, hoping that nothing was out of place.

'You need not worry, child,' said Lady Bedlington. 'You look utterly charming.'

'Thank you.'

'Ah, and I think my great nephew thinks so too.'

'He is here?' Calista looked towards the door and saw the Colonel arriving. He was dressed in black, and whereas most of the other men wore knee breaches and garters, he wore the new style of drainpipe trousers made famous by Beau Brummell. Calista could not help thinking that it made him look more masculine than the other men.

'You seem surprised, child.'

'Only because yesterday he told me that he did not care for society, so I did not think he would come to a place like this.'

'Perhaps he has good reason.'

The Colonel walked across to them, and as he did, Calista saw that nearly every woman's eyes followed his progress.

'Good evening, Brook. Miss Haywood was just saying that she did not expect to see you here.'

The colonel smiled. 'Normally I cannot abide these gatherings, but I wanted to witness Miss Haywood's first official step into society. How are you finding it, Miss Haywood?'

'Rather overwhelming at the moment,' said Calista. 'I'm terrified of saying and doing the wrong thing.'

'I am sure you would never do either. Would you like to dance? Or is your dance card already filled?'

It was on Calista's lips to say that even if it were, she would make a space for him. Instead she said, 'I think all the young men are waiting to see if my step-sister is available first.'

'Then their loss is my gain.'

'This should be interesting,' said Lady Bedlington, wryly. 'I have never seen you dance, Brook.'

'I'll have you know I'm famed for my dancing, Aunt Agatha. Though not necessarily for good reasons.'

The dances in Almacks were mostly square dances or country jigs, so there was not much chance to talk to the Colonel. All Calista knew was that each time she took his hand to do a turn, a thrill ran through her. She could feel the heat emanating through his gloves and hers. She wished that no one else would ask her to dance all night, and that he could be her only partner. Despite his joke, he danced very well.

As soon as the dance ended, other young men began to flock around her, quickly filling up her dance card. She kept one space empty at the end, hoping that the Colonel might ask her again so that the evening might end as enjoyably as it started. While she was dancing with others, she was acutely aware of his eyes following her, as he stood next to his great aunt's chair, and was surprised to see that he did not ask any other ladies to dance. Some of them fluttered around him, speaking in hopeful tones, but after a few polite words from him, they moved away.

'I am so charmed to meet you, Miss Haywood,' said one young man, whose name she had missed.

'That is very kind. Thank you.' The dance was slower, so she and the young man had more chance to talk.

'Tell me, do you know if your step-sister's dance card is full yet?' And that was when Calista realized that the young men dancing with her really were only waiting their turn with Blanche. 'I have no idea, sir. Perhaps you should ask her.'

'Yes, yes, I should really. But . . . she is so exquisite. So unreachable. I dare not.'

'She does not bite,' said Calista with a smile. Even as she said it, she doubted her own words. 'I am sure she will be delighted to dance with you.'

'Purbeck is monopolizing her. It's really a bad show, don't you know? One is supposed to circulate at these events.'

That explained why the Colonel had not asked Calista for another dance. At least she hoped that was the reason. 'They say he will be the next Duke of Midchester,' the young man continued. 'Old Midchester picks up and drops favourites at the drop of a hat. Everyone knows that. My brother was a favourite last year, but then the fool went and married an actress. I ask you.' The young man droned on in that vein throughout the dance, so that by the time it ended, Calista breathed a sigh of relief.

She had one dance left on her card, and looked hopefully towards the Colonel. But his eyes were fixed on a spot at the far end of the room. She saw his great aunt reach up and put her hand on his arm, as if to stop him from saying or doing something.

Glancing in the direction he was staring, Calista saw that Blanche was pushing Mr. Purbeck forward. She could not hear what Blanche was saying but it seemed to be along the lines of, 'Just do it.'

Purbeck crossed the room to where the Colonel stood. 'A word with you, sir.'

'You may have as many words as you wish, Mr. Purbeck.'

'You dishonored my sister, sir.' Purbeck's tones became louder, more petulant. The music ground to a halt and everyone stopped dancing and turned to listen.

'I do not think so.'

'I should like to call you out on it, sir.'

From across the room, Calista could see Blanche's eyes shining with excitement.

'Might I remind you, Mr. Purbeck, that dueling is now illegal. I did not dishonor your sister. In fact, I believe I did her the honour of letting her marry the man she really loved rather than insisting on her keeping her promise to me.'

'Purbeck!' Everyone turned to where a man in his late fifties stood watching the exchange. Even without being told, Calista knew it was the Duke of Midchester. He was as handsome as his son, apart from the fact that his mouth was set in a cruel line, and his grey eyes were as hard and cold as flint. She wondered that no one else saw the similarity but reasoned that people generally saw what they wanted to see.

'Your Grace,' Purbeck stammered. 'I did not realize you would be here tonight.'

'You should remember who is your patron, Mr. Purbeck, and upon whose good graces you depend. Do not waste your time and your reputation on the . . . the nouveau riche.' The duke spat the last words out as if they were an obscenity.

There was a gasp of horror around the room. The nouveau riche were not permitted through Almacks' doors. One might be as poor as a church mouse and get in as long as one were of the nobility. But new money was considered vulgar.

The Countess of Jersey, one of the patronesses, stepped forward and in quiet but urgent tones spoke to the Duke. He muttered something back to her, at which point she walked to where the Colonel stood. Another muttered conversation took place, after which the colonel stormed across the room and left Almacks.

'No!' said Calista, blushing when she realized that everyone turned to look at her.

'Calista,' said Lady Bedlington, beckoning to her. 'Come to me, child.' The tender use of her Christian name surprised Calista into silence. Lady Bedlington spoke to the room in general. 'I am afraid Miss Haywood is distressed by the events. I will take her to another room and help calm her nerves.' When Calista had joined her and they were walking along a corridor, Lady Bedlington said, 'I told you being here required a strong drink.' At which point she took a flask from her reticule and drank from it.

'I do not understand why he has been ejected,' said Calista when she and Lady Bedlington were alone in one of the comfortably furnished private sitting rooms. 'It is unfair. He is of the nobility, is he not? On his mother's side.'

'Yes, child, but you must not assume he has been ejected. He may have chosen to leave.'

'Why would he?'

'To prevent a scandal. So as not to spoil . . . someone's . . . evening.'

'It is not fair. Mr. Purbeck should be the one to leave. He shamed himself by his behaviour.'

'Urged, I gather, by your step-sister.'

'Yes. Yes, that is true and I am sorry . . .'

'Calista, why are you apologizing for her behaviour? It is not your fault. I was merely stating a fact.'

'We are related. Even if only by marriage.'

'Hmm. That is unfortunate for you, I fear. I am afraid your step-sister got rather ahead of herself. She believed that one visit to Almacks meant that she had made society. But the patronesses can just as easily take a voucher back. I suspect she liked the idea of men dueling over her, but as Brook has treated her with nothing but civility, she had to content herself with persuading Purbeck to duel about his sister.'

'Did the Colonel love her very much?' asked Calista.

Lady Bedlington looked at her thoughtfully. 'I do not know, child. She was a flighty girl. And is apparently a flighty woman. Brook would not be told, but then young people never do listen. He did not lie when he said he paid her the honour of letting her marry the man she truly loved. Or at least the man she loved at that time. He could have made much more fuss about it and with good reason. She played them off against each other. Much as I think your step-sister is doing with Mr. Purbeck and my nephew at this moment.' Lady Bedlington went over to the fireplace and tugged on the bell.

Almost immediately a servant arrived. 'Tell Mrs. Haywood and Miss Kirkham that I should like to see them both here immediately.'

When Evelyn and Blanche arrived several minutes later, Blanche was flushed with excitement. 'Is there a problem?' she asked. 'I am rather enjoying myself and did not wish to leave the dance.'

'Yes, Miss Kirkham,' said Lady Bedlington. 'There is a problem. Shut the door please. I am going to say this in front of your mother and step-sister so that I have witnesses.'

'Lady Bedlington, I . . . ' Evelyn got no further before Lady Bedlington raised her hand.

'Do not make any more excuses for

your daughter, Mrs. Haywood. You are a good woman and your loyalty does you credit. I think you have struggled to try to be fair. That too does you credit. I, however, do not have to be fair. Sit down, Miss Kirkham. You will not like what I have to say.'

Blanche looked as though she might argue, but instead took a seat on the sofa next to Calista.

'You may think,' Lady Bedlington began, 'that by being allowed through the doors of Almacks that you are now a part of society. It is unfortunate then that you failed the test on your first evening here. I saw you goading Mr. Purbeck to challenge my nephew . . . ' Lady Bedlington held up her hand again. 'Do not deny it, child. Others may be fooled by you, but I am not. Now you may be here because of the Duke of Midchester. It does amuse him to tease the young women whom Purbeck fools into believing he will be the next Duke, just as much as it amuses him to tease his favourites into believing he will name them his successors. But you are a guest in my home, and everyone here is aware of that. I have a great regard for your dear mother but I warn you now that if you behave in such an outrageous way again whilst my guest, whether you are under my roof at the time or not, I will send you back to Derbyshire. And I can assure you that once I have ejected you from my house, no one else will invite you to stay. Is that clear?'

'Believe me, Lady Bedlington,' said Blanche, looking panic-stricken, 'I tried to stop Mr. Purbeck. Truly I did. But he believed the Colonel had insulted me.'

'I wonder whatever gave him that idea.'

'I do not know. I only mentioned that I thought the Colonel did not like me very much. It is something I cannot put my finger upon. So Mr. Purbeck decided instead to bring up the subject of his sister when really he meant to defend me.'

'And is Mr. Purbeck to challenge

everyone who does not like you? Because if he is, then I fear he will be up at the crack of dawn every day for the rest of his life.'

'That is very harsh, Lady Bedlington.' Tears filled Blanche's eyes, and unaccountably, Calista felt sorry for her. It is hurtful to be told one is not liked.

'Yes,' said Evelyn, clearly feeling she had to defend her daughter. 'Yes, Lady Bedlington, with all due respect, that is rather harsh. I understand your anger, but my daughter is very young and made a young woman's mistake.'

'Perhaps it was harsh, and perhaps I am now sorry I said it. But your daughter needs to learn two things. Humility and how to behave in polite society. I do not blame you, Evelyn.' Lady Bedlington's voice became kinder. 'Your manners are impeccable, as are Calista's. Though even she is prone to emotional outbursts when she feels strongly about something.' Calista blushed, but saw that Lady Bedlington was smiling kindly at her. 'Blanche would do well to study from you both. Believe me, if Miss Kirkham does not hear the truth from me, in the privacy of this room, and does not take note, she will hear it in public, and I can assure you, much harsher things will be said of her. I am sure you do not wish that to happen. So as unkind as I may seem, I am in fact rendering your daughter a kindness in being so candid at such an early stage in her social life.'

'We thank you for your candid words. Blanche, do you have something to say to Lady Bedlington?'

'I humbly apologise for my behaviour, Lady Bedlington.'

'Very well. Nothing that has been said in this room will be repeated by me, or anyone else, outside of it, and we will all leave here as friends. Now, if you will excuse me, I must go and freshen up.'

They curtseyed to Lady Bedlington and she left the room, reaching into her reticule as she did so.

The moment the old lady left the room, Blanche's humble demeanour changed. 'I hate her, and I hate you two. When I am the Duchess of Midchester, she will be thrown out of society. I will make it my life's work to make sure that happens. As for you two, you always preferred it in Derbyshire anyway.'

'Blanche,' said Calista, feeling as if the cold hand of gloom gripped her heart. 'Blanche, please listen to what she says. She is only trying to be helpful.'

'Oh, but you are her pet. Everyone can see that. You think everything she does is wonderful. No doubt trying to keep on the good side of her nouveau riche nephew.'

'I am sorry that her harsh words caused you pain,' said Calista, keeping her anger under control. 'Even if you do not believe it to be so. You are very well liked, I am sure. All the young men I danced with preferred to be with you.'

'I do not need you to patronize me, Calista.' Even so, there was a look of triumph in Blanche's eyes.

'I wasn't . . . I . . . '

Blanche was not listening. She swept

out of the room with a regal gait.

'Oh Calista,' said Evelyn, sinking down onto the sofa and putting her head in her hands. 'I have never been so ashamed in my life.'

Calista knelt at Evelyn's feet. 'It was just high spirits, I am sure.'

'But the way she spoke about ruining Lady Bedlington's standing in society. I do believe she means it. I am afraid, Calista, desperately afraid. For her, for you, for me.'

'I do not think you need be afraid for Lady Bedlington's standing in society,' said Calista with a smile. 'I have no doubt she can hold her own. I also suspect she does not care much more for society than her great nephew.'

'People only say that until they're faced with the fear of losing their standing in the Ton,' said Evelyn. Her eyes had a faraway look. 'If Blanche knew how much she had to lose . . . '

'What do you mean?'

'Nothing. I am being silly. Nothing bad will happen. And if we are exiled back to Derbyshire, I for one will not be sorry. Will you?'

'No, no of course not.'

'Except,' Evelyn said perceptively, 'there is no Colonel Windebank in Derbyshire.'

'Or Mr. Benedict,' Calista teased. Instead of smiling back, Evelyn's face took on a look of doom again.

'Please tell me what troubles you,' said Calista.

'I sometimes feel that if I do not tell someone I shall explode,' said Evelyn. 'But I am afraid, Calista. You are a good, honourable girl and I have enjoyed having you as my daughter. I fear that if I tell you the truth about myself, I will lose your love and affection.'

'Nothing could make that happen, I swear it.'

Evelyn took a deep breath and seemed to come to a decision. 'Very well. But I will tell you when we return to Lady Bedlington's. I fear we may be overheard here.'

They returned home in the early

hours of the morning. Blanche swept past everyone and announced she was going to bed. Evelyn and Calista had a brief conversation with Lady Bedlington about the ball, avoiding the more emotional parts of the evening. Evelyn bid them goodnight, and Calista was about to leave when Lady Bedlington called her back.

'What is it?'

'Sit down, child.'

Calista did as she was told. 'Have I done something wrong? If it is about my outburst . . . '

Lady Bedlington smiled and held up her hand to stop Calista. 'You did nothing wrong. I just want to be sure about one thing.'

'What is that?'

'That you are as much in love with my nephew as I believe you to be.'

'I . . . I would not presume to . . . what I mean is . . . I know he could never love someone like me. So please do not think I am out to trap him or anything like that.'

'I did not suggest any such thing. But I think you have just answered my question anyway.' The truth was that Calista had not known it herself until Lady Bedlington asked her. The realization hit her like a tornado, churning up her emotions, and also terrifying her. 'I only asked,' continued Lady Bedlington, 'because my nephew has known a lot of pain in his life. I do not want to see him hurt again.'

'Would you prefer it if I went away? I could return to Derbyshire tomorrow.'

'No, child. Whatever made you think such a thing?'

'I thought you disapproved.'

'Believe me, if I did you would know about it. I just need to know that I can trust you, Calista. Because I am afraid.'

Calista looked at Lady Bedlington wide-eyed. She had spoken the exact same words as Evelyn. Calista had put her step-mother's words down to nervousness and shame over Blanche's behaviour. Now she truly understood that malevolence crackled in the air.

Lady Bedlington had also picked up on it.

'I must protect you, child,' said Lady Bedlington. 'And between us, we must protect Brook. He is more vulnerable than he realizes. Can I count on you?'

'Yes, of course, I would do anything to protect him.'

6

'I just want to assure you of one more thing before you go to bed,' said Lady Bedlington. Calista had risen from the sofa and was halfway to the door.

'What is that?'

'Whatever might happen in the future, child, you are not without friends or protection. You may always come to me. Remember that.'

'Do you mean if Evelyn marries Mr. Benedict and Papa's annuity ends?'

Lady Bedlington did not answer for a long time. She just looked tired and old. 'Yes, I suppose that is what I mean.'

Calista was grateful to go up to bed. She needed time to think over what had been said. Only she remembered that Evelyn had promised to speak to her. She knocked quietly on her step-mother's bedroom door.

'Come in, Calista.'

Evelyn was sitting up in bed. She too looked tired, but she also looked very beautiful. 'I'm sorry I kept you waiting,' said Calista. She went to sit on the edge of the bed.

'I understand. One does not ignore a command from Lady Bedlington. I cannot always work her out. One moment she is all kindness. The next . . . well, she has the sting of a scorpion. Though I do believe her kindness always wins out. What did she wish to see you about? Or is that yet another secret you are sworn to keep?'

'I do not think it is a secret. She is afraid of something, as you are. Anything other than that, I cannot tell you. It is rather nebulous, and yet . . . '

'And yet you do not doubt her fears.'

'No. Nor yours. If you are tired, I could come back in the morning.' For reasons Calista could not fathom, suddenly she did not want to know Evelyn's secret. The truth was a frightening prospect. The truth, she felt, might tear their lives apart, though she had no idea why that might be.

'You do not want to know?'

'Yes, of course.' Calista took Evelyn's hand in hers. 'Of course, but only if you wish to tell me.'

'It is rather a long story. Or perhaps it is not. I could just blurt out a simple fact and have it over with. Only . . . only I want you to understand that I did not feel at the time that I did anything wrong. I was in love.'

'With Mr. Benedict?'

'Yes. With Mr. Benedict. Harry and I grew up together. We were childhood sweethearts, with all the innocent pursuits that entails. Then . . . ' Evelyn paused. 'Then we were not so innocent. I was seventeen and he was eighteen and we were in love. Nothing seemed wrong then. Can you understand that? Regardless of what society says, or what the bible says, nothing seemed wrong to us. Because we loved each other. Do you understand what I'm trying to tell you?'

'I think so,' said Calista.

'But Harry had to go away to university and I did not want to hold him back. He is every bit as talented an architect as your father. So he went off to Oxford. I waited for him to write to me, but he did not. I sent him dozens of notes, declaring my love, but heard nothing. When my father announced that Mr. Kirkham had asked for my hand in marriage, I agreed. More out of anger than anything. I was sure Harry had forgotten about me and found a new love. Or perhaps lots of new loves. So I married Mr. Kirkham. Even then, with everything that had happened, I was an innocent. So when I found out I was expecting Blanche, I told my husband, thinking he would be pleased. Sadly he was better at arithmetic than I was.'

'What do you mean?'

Evelyn lowered her voice. 'I mean Blanche could not possibly be his child. She is Harry's.'

'Oh.'

'Now I have lost you.'

'No, please do not think that. I am surprised, but not shocked or outraged. You must have loved Mr. Benedict very much.'

'I did. Of course, my husband could not divorce me without bringing shame upon himself. But he never let me forget my own shame, and he never . . . I feel embarrassed telling you this, considering I have told you so much. He never touched me again. In public he would be a doting husband, but at home I would have to endure a dozen slights every day. That is the atmosphere in which Blanche grew up. She has no respect for me, because her father, perhaps reasonably, had no respect for me.'

'I am so sorry you've suffered so much.'

'Not always. I want you to know that I did not deceive your father. When he asked for my hand in marriage, I told him the truth about everything. I was sure he would say he did not want to marry me. When he said it did not matter, I still refused, convinced he would change once we were married. He remained constant and true, asking me time and again to be his wife. So much so that what was a fondness for him changed to deep and abiding love. He never betrayed that love by treating me cruelly after we married. I can honestly say that the few years I spent with your father were amongst the happiest of my life.'

'I am glad. Papa loved you as you deserve to be loved. No one should have to suffer for one mistake.'

'Sadly it is not only I who will suffer if anyone ever finds out. Now you can perhaps understand why Mr. Benedict's reappearance in my life was not a good thing. If the truth ever came out, Blanche might be ruined. All her hopes and dreams of being a duchess shattered.'

'How would anyone ever find out?'

'I do not know, Calista. But even Lady Bedlington knows that Harry and

I were childhood sweethearts, and I am sure others are also better at arithmetic than I was. And now you know.'

'I would never betray you.'

'No, I know that, dearest. That is why I knew I could tell you. Please promise me that this has not changed the way you feel about me.'

'Not at all. I am only sorry that your life was so sad until you met Papa. Does Mr. Benedict know?'

'No!' Evelyn looked startled. 'No, and he must never know.'

'Has he given any explanation as to why he did not write to you? Because I have seen the way he looks at you, and he clearly has a high regard for you.'

'We managed to speak about it only this morning. I made a joke of it, telling him that his letter-writing skills were not very good. He says that he wrote many times and that he was heart-broken when he heard that I married another. The funny thing is, I believe him. I now think that my father hid the letters, as he had found what he thought was a better match.'

'I really do not see why you cannot be together,' said Calista. 'If you love each other.'

'I have been lucky enough to know happiness twice in my life, Calista. Once with Harry when I was very young, and once with your father. I do not deceive myself that at my age I can find such happiness again. Perhaps now I am truly being punished for my youthful behaviour.'

'Do not say that, Evelyn. Why only the other day you and I were saying that we should both find happiness again. Have you forgotten already?'

'No, I have not forgotten, but that certainty has been replaced by a fear of something bad happening.'

'Lady Bedlington said much the same thing. Now I feel it. A darkness descending over us.' So dark in fact, that for a moment Calista thought she sensed it lurking just beyond the bedroom door, waiting to creep in. She shook her head to eradicate the gloom. 'And we are all being silly. It has been a long, stressful day and we are all tired. Tomorrow will bring a better day and happier feelings. I know it.'

'I hope so.' Evelyn smiled sadly.

Calista went to her own room and started to undress. She had told the maid to go to bed, feeling guilty about keeping the poor girl up so late. For the first time since she had met her step-sister, she started thinking of her as 'poor Blanche'. No child should have to live with the stigma of being illegitimate, especially in such a hypo-critical society. Calista knew of girls from their town who had to go away, returning many months later looking older and sadder. Some had been sent away from their parents' homes perma-nently.

A few months earlier, she admitted to herself, she might have been shocked at Evelyn's youthful behaviour, although she hoped she would always be sympa-thetic. Now, because she loved the Colonel, she understood how Evelyn must have felt about Mr. Benedict. The Colonel only had to touch her hand, and through her glove at that, for her to long for his touch to linger and to turn into something more passionate. At night she had fevered dreams about him, from which she awoke excited, but also blushing furiously.

She could easily understand how such feelings and emotions could overwhelm a woman so that she forgot to behave properly and just gave in to the desire. Evelyn and Mr. Benedict should have been allowed to marry. Then there would be no secret shame. It was reprehensible of her father to have prevented it by withholding the letters, and reprehensible for Mr. Kirkham to treat Evelyn so badly because of it. Calista had no doubt that there had been other women for Mr. Kirkham before he married. Young men were expected to know all about women. Sadly double standards ruled the day.

On the other hand, Calista thought more charitably, if Mr. Kirkham loved

Evelyn then it must have been hurtful to him to learn that she had not only given her heart, but also her body, to another man. She could still not believe that justified him treating her so cruelly over the years. There was such a thing as forgiveness.

She wondered if Blanche really would be ruined by such a revelation and conceded that she might well be. Perhaps it would not have been before their visit to Almacks. Her behaviour with Purbeck at the ball had already shown her in a bad light. The truth of her birth might at the very least be one more strike against her in the society to which she so desperately aspired. It would also ruin Evelyn, and that was something that Calista did not want to see happen.

'Life is not fair,' she said out loud as she climbed into bed. 'People are not fair.' She sent up a silent prayer that Evelyn would be safe from censure and that one day she might be able to marry Mr. Benedict.

Then, as happened so many times last thing at night, Calista's thoughts turned to the Colonel. She began to wonder why Lady Bedlington thought he might be in danger. He was a man who was more than capable of taking care of himself, of that Calista had no doubt. She wondered where he had gone when he left Almacks. He had not returned to Lady Bedlington's as far as she knew.

Instead of going to sleep as she intended, she went to the window and curled up in the window seat, looking out in the hopes of seeing him return. With her head rested on the cool window pane, she began to doze.

It was much later still when she became vaguely aware of being carried in strong arms to her bed, and then covered with a blanket. She was sure she dreamed it all, including the gentle kiss on her lips that followed. She awoke the next morning and found that she was indeed in bed, with no memory of having got into it herself.

At breakfast, which they took in their sitting room, Blanche was surprisingly cheerful, and even more surprisingly, attentive to her mother. 'Let me pour your tea, Mama dearest,' she said, picking up the teapot. 'Would you like some honey for your bread? No, I shall spread it for you. There.'

'Thank you, dear,' said Evelyn. Whilst Calista was immediately suspicious about Blanche's sudden ministrations, Evelyn seemed relieved. 'You are in good spirits this morning.'

'Love has softened me, Mama. I understand now how you felt about Mr. Haywood, and I wish to apologise for my unkindness. To you too, Calista. I had no idea that love could be so overwhelming, so all-encompassing. Why, I could become a poet!'

'I'm glad you're happy,' said Calista, hiding her own reservations. 'Are we to assume Mr. Purbeck is the lucky man?'

'Why, of course! Who else?'

'You danced with a lot of handsome men at the ball last night. Anyone of them might have won your heart.'

'You do say nice things, Calista. However, despite my popularity at the ball, it is indeed Mr. Purbeck who has my heart. Our shared troubles have brought us closer together. And you need not worry. I have written to him this morning, censuring him for his hot-headed behaviour with the Colonel and demanding that he apologise.'

'So are all your thoughts of revenge gone?' asked Calista.

Blanche laughed heartily at that. 'I was embarrassed and ashamed last night, so do not know what silly things I may have uttered in the heat of the moment. As if I could have any bearing on Lady Bedlington's standing in society. No, I have had time to think and reflect and I realize that, as she so wisely said, she was paying me a kindness in being blunt with me. The truth does hurt, I admit that, but I hope it has done me some good too.'

'I am glad to hear it,' said Evelyn. 'I know you are a good girl at heart,

Blanche, and today you have proved it. Has she not, Calista?'

'Yes. Oh yes, certainly.' Calista was anything but certain. Blanche was never kind or nice to anyone, and in many ways Calista preferred that as she knew what she was dealing with. This new Blanche was a mystery, and as such rather frightening. 'Could you pass the honey, please, Blanche?'

Normally Blanche would tell Calista to get her own honey. 'Of course . . . ' As Blanche lifted up the pot it slipped from her hand, crashing to the floor and spilling the contents. 'Oh, what a fool I am. Calista, be a dear and call the maid, will you? We need more honey. Come on, Mama, eat up or we shall never be ready to go out walking.'

'Now there's the Blanche we know and love,' said Evelyn, with a smile.

'Mama, you are such a tease.'

Calista was not smiling. Despite Blanche's apparent volte face, she was still gripped by a sense of unease. She had no doubt at all that her step-sister had meant every word she said the night before about bringing Lady Bedlington down. She had spoken with cold, calculating anger, not a sudden rush of fury because she felt embarrassed and ashamed. It could only be assumed, by Calista at least, even if Evelyn was fooled, that Blanche had a new game plan.

There was not much chance to speak to Evelyn alone. The maid arrived to clean up the mess and take away the breakfast things. Then Blanche was eager to go. 'I have ordered a new ball gown, Mama,' she said. 'I am told it will be ready this morning.'

'Blanche, I told you we could not afford anything else. Is this why you are being nice to me?'

'Mama, you hurt me with your distrust. I told you, I have learned my lesson. Would not a new dress show that you forgive me?'

'We shall have to see, Blanche. It depends how much it costs. Also, it is not fair that you should have one when

Calista does not.'

Before anyone could answer, there was a knock on the door. It was the Colonel.

'Good morning. I hope I am not intruding.'

'Not at all, Colonel,' said Evelyn. 'We were just about to go out walking.'

'I am here to extend an invitation. The King is holding a ball at St. James's Palace tomorrow night and . . . '

'Oh, Mama,' Blanche said, clapping her hands together. 'I told you that I would need a new ball gown.'

'Forgive me for misleading you, Miss Kirkham. The invitation is for myself, my aunt and one guest. I had hoped that Miss Haywood would join us.'

'Oh.' Calista put her hands to her face. 'I do not think I could possibly go without Blanche and Evelyn.'

'And you, Miss Kirkham,' said the Colonel pointedly, 'would you have such scruples if the invitation included you?'

'Of course,' said Blanche, coldly.

'And I agree dear Calista must go. Hopefully there will be no one there who saw her dress last night.' Blanche swept from the room, closely followed by Evelyn.

'Then it is settled,' said the Colonel. 'You will come with us.'

'I am not sure,' said Calista. She could not help feeling that the Colonel had deliberately worded the invitation to allow Blanche to think she was included. Had he merely done so to get back at her step-sister for the trouble she had caused him the night before?

7

'The King does not normally like having his invitations refused.'

'I am sure that as the King only said you could bring a guest, he would have no idea I have refused the invitation.'

'And what about me? I know you have refused.'

'I do not know,' said Calista, frowning. She wanted to ask him, but did not want to seem ungrateful for the invitation. 'I do not wish to cause offence, but . . . '

'You do not want to go with me?'

'That is not it, Colonel. I suppose I just feel guilty about Blanche. She has longed to meet the King.'

'And no doubt would encourage young Purbeck to challenge him to a duel if she thinks the King does not like her.'

Calista could not help smiling at that.

She doubted even the foolish Purbeck would dare do such a thing.

'Please say you will come, Calista.' His voice was gentle and seductive. 'My great aunt is very eager to present you to the King.'

How could Calista explain to him that seeing the King did not really matter? Only the chance to spend another evening in the Colonel's company excited her. If only she did not have so many doubts as to why he had asked her. If only she had the courage to ask him, but she feared causing offence if she were wrong. It was not the sort of thing one blurted out when such a kind invitation had been given. Added to which, she was confused because of her feelings for him. She did not trust her own responses if he replied that, yes, he had only done it to teach Blanche a lesson. She might break down in tears in front of him, and then he would no doubt despise her.

'I'm waiting for your answer,' he said.

'Thank you for your kind invitation. I

would like to meet the King.' Let him think that was her only interest in the evening. That way she would not be laying herself open to him.

His eyes narrowed slightly. 'Good. Then it is settled. I have to spend the day at my house, working on the plans with Mr. Benedict. I will see you at dinner tonight, perhaps.' He bowed and went towards the door, then turned back. 'If I have said something to offend you, Calista, then I am sorry. Or perhaps it was because of last night?'

'Last night?'

'With my father calling me nouveau riche. No doubt it made you think differently about me.'

'No. Not at all. I do not see why it even matters.'

'It does in Almacks. And in most of what we call society.'

'Is that why you left?'

'No, I left because Lady DeVilliers asked me to, to help defuse the situation. One thing I learned in the army is that sometimes one has to know when to retreat and when to advance.'

'It was not fair that you should have to leave and Purbeck did not.'

'He's a hot-headed child. Such behaviour in him is more forgivable than it would have been in a man of my age. Though he is now on borrowed time. He will not survive many more such outbursts.'

'That is what your great aunt said to Blanche.'

'She is right. Already people are talking about it, and her name is connected. They were even talking about it when I went to St James' Palace last night.'

'Is that where you went? After you left Almacks?'

'Yes. That was when the King invited me to the ball. Why?'

'Oh. No reason. I just . . . ' Calista could not admit to him that she had sat at the window for ages waiting for him to return. 'I just wondered, that's all.'

The Colonel smiled. 'I see. Were you worried about me, Calista?'

'I hardly think you need anyone to

worry about you, Colonel.'

'Everyone needs at least one person in their life who waits at the window for them.'

Blushing furiously, Calista stared after him wide-eyed as he took his leave.

Calista, Evelyn and Blanche had their coats on and were about to leave for their walk, when they were summoned by Lady Bedlington. Unusually for such an early hour, Her Ladyship was up and dressed.

'I am glad I caught you,' she said. 'Evelyn, I wish to make a gift to you and the two young ladies.'

'Your hospitality is enough,' said Evelyn.

'That is very kind. But I still wish to make a gift and I shall be offended if you refuse. What I thought was that I would buy you all a brand-new ball gown.'

'Lady Bedlington, really . . . That is a very kind offer. Only it seems rather a lot . . . '

'As I said, Evelyn, I shall be offended if you refuse. After last night's unpleasantness, I wish to do something to show that we are all friends again.'

'It is most generous,' said Blanche, her eyes shining.

'Thank you,' said Calista, wondering what had brought about Lady Bedlington's sudden rush of generosity. Then again, she had already been generous in giving them a roof over their heads for the Season and making sure they met the right people.

'What I suggest,' Lady Bedlington continued, 'is that you, Evelyn, and Miss Kirkham go on ahead to the shops and order your dresses. Tell the dressmakers to add the bill to my account. If Miss Haywood will be kind enough to wait for me, she can accompany me in my carriage.'

Whilst it seemed a strange request, Evelyn and Blanche agreed, leaving soon after.

'That was very clever of me, do you not think, Calista?' said Lady Bedlington.

'I am not sure what you mean.'

'I mean that I wished to buy you a new dress for the ball at St. James's

Palace but I did not want to put Blanche's nose out of joint as, I gather, my great nephew did earlier.'

Calista did not feel comfortable enough with Lady Bedlington to ask if she thought the Colonel was merely trying to get back at Blanche. 'You really do not have to buy me a dress. Unless . . . well unless you think the one I have will not be good enough for St. James's Palace.'

'It is a perfectly suitable and charming dress. However Brook mentioned that it seemed unfair to him that Blanche was to have a new gown and you were not, so I said I would buy you one. And it seemed to me that things would be much worse for you if I left Blanche out. Now, let us go and purchase your gown. Then we will dine out for luncheon.'

The morning was spent in a flurry of activity, as Lady Bedlington took Calista first to a dressmaker, then to a milliner and then on to luncheon at a fine restaurant. Calista could not help noticing that the dressmaker was not the same one that Blanche used, despite Lady Bedlington saying they would meet them at some point.

'I thought we were only buying a ball gown,' said Calista when they sat down to luncheon.

'You do not like your new morning dress?'

'I like it very much, only . . . '

'Do you think your step-sister notices anything you wear, Calista?' asked Lady Bedlington.

'No, I do not suppose she does.'

'Then the extra dress will be our secret.'

'I think she might notice it is finer than all my other clothes,' said Calista with a smile. 'I am very grateful,' she added hastily. Not only had Lady Bedlington bought her two new gowns, but also new under garments and other accessories such as ribbons and bows, and a reticule to match her ball gown. All Calista could do was obey meekly as Her Ladyship gave orders to the dressmaker and milliner to measure her.

Despite her reservations about accepting the clothes, she could not deny the pleasure of choosing new gowns and accessories. Or at least choosing as far as she were allowed. Lady Bedlington knew instinctively what was right for Calista and was not shy about sending the dressmaker back to find something more suitable. When the dressmaker emerged with one particularly bright-coloured gown, Lady Bedlington snapped, 'You are dressing a decent, well-bred young woman, not an actress.' The tradespeople were clearly terrified of her, and she seemed to actively enjoy their fear, having them scurrying all over the shop to find the correct attire. 'When you get to my age,' she had murmured to Calista, 'tormenting tradespeople is one of the few pleasures in life.'

And yet, despite Lady Bedlington's sometimes waspish tongue, everyone seemed to adore her. Perhaps because she was never unfairly sharp. She would often follow up a tongue-lashing with a charming and well-deserved compliment, to the point that it was sometimes impossible to see the join.

It was the same in the restaurant. There were other diners there, some of whom Calista recognized as being higher up the nobility than Lady Bedlington. Yet it was for her that the waiters dashed around, making sure everything was perfect. She rewarded them with a dazzling smile and, before they left, a big tip. The other diners also came up to talk to her whilst they awaited their food.

One man, a rather jowly nobleman in his fifties, came over to the table, his legs wobbling dangerously as if he had had far too much to drink. 'So, Agatha, who is this young filly?'

'This is my relative, Calista Haywood. Calista, this is the Earl of Garwood.'

'I'm pleased to meet you, My Lord,' said Calista. She felt uncomfortable under his scrutiny, and only vaguely noticed Lady Bedlington describing her as a relative.

'And I am very pleased to meet you, young lady.' The Earl leered at her, still rocking back and for on his toes. 'What brings you to London? Husband-hunting no doubt. Well, I'm looking to take a new wife. May I call on you tomorrow?'

'I . . . er . . . ' Calista looked at Lady Bedlington, terrified of saying the wrong thing, but knowing that she did not want anything to do with this horrible, drunken man.

'You may not,' said Lady Bedlington.

'Let the girl answer for herself, can't you?' said the Earl.

'Calista has not yet reached her majority, so any protestations of affection you wish to show will have to come via me. I assure you, I intend to choose very well for my little cousin.'

'Dash it, Agatha, I am on ten thousand a year, and have a title. She could not do much better.' The Earl looked at Calista. 'You would do well to consider my offer, girl.' He wandered away from their table, and almost crashed into a group of diners at another table.

'I do not want to marry him,' Calista whispered. She was gripped by the fear that if Lady Bedlington decided it was a good match, then she would have no choice but to say yes, out of gratitude for what Her Ladyship had done for her.

'Of course not. He's an old man, and a drunk at that. Do not look so afraid. He asks a dozen women a week to marry him when he is drunk. No doubt he will wake up tomorrow morning and forget having asked you. Ah, here is someone to put the smile back on your face.'

Calista turned in the direction that Lady Bedlington was looking and saw the Colonel walking towards them. 'You are late, Brook.'

'I'm sorry Aunt Agatha . . . Miss Haywood. The work on the house has just started and I wanted to be sure that the builders know what they are doing. Mr. Benedict is supervising them now.'

'Well come and sit down and order, otherwise we shall never eat.'

The Colonel sat between Calista and Lady Bedlington, and was immediately given a menu. 'Has everything been sorted out?' he said to his aunt.

'Yes.'

'Good.'

'Sorted out?' said Calista.

'Just some private business between us, dear girl,' said Lady Bedlington.

'Oh. I am sorry. I did not mean to pry.'

'You had every right to. It is ill-mannered of Brook to start a conversation in which you can have no part.'

'Yes, it was,' said the Colonel. 'Please accept my apologies, Miss Haywood.'

'May I ask you what changes you decided upon in the house?' asked Calista, assaulted by the intense feeling that she wanted to change the subject. Although she could not be certain, she had a feeling that the cryptic conversation between the Colonel and his great aunt had something to do with her and also that it had something to do with her new dresses.

Was it possible that the Colonel had insisted she be better attired for the ball at St. James's Palace? And if so, did that mean that he had noticed her clothes and found her wanting?

'Aren't you longing to tell me all about your new ball gown and pretty new hat?' said the Colonel, his lips forming into a wry grin.

'I am sure you would find that very boring,' said Calista.

'He is teasing you, Calista. Take no notice. Now tell Calista all about your house or I shall send you home at once.'

'Actually I won't,' said the Colonel. 'I want it to be a surprise. I've already promised Miss Haywood she can be amongst my first guests.'

Calista was about to answer, when she noticed the Earl of Garton approaching them again. 'So this is the way the wind is blowing, is it, girly?' he said to her.

'I am not sure I understand what you mean.'

'You've got your eye on this young upstart.'

The Colonel stood up slowly, standing a full head and shoulders taller than the Earl. 'I think you are in your cups, sir,' said the Colonel. 'And as such are causing my great aunt and Miss Haywood offence. I suggest you go and sleep it off.'

'Your days are numbered,' said the Earl. 'Everyone is talking about what happened at Almacks and how the Duke of Midchester denounced you as nouveau riche. Soon you will not be welcome anywhere.'

'You say that as if it matters, Lord Garton. To me it does not. However, I am sure that for you it does matter, so I suggest you behave with more propriety in future.'

The Earl was outclassed and he probably knew it, but before he left, he had one more volley. 'Do not think, Windebank, that His Majesty's admiration for your war record will protect you forever. He is, as you know, notoriously fickle with his friendship.'

'Once again,' said the Colonel, coldly, 'you say that as if it matters.'

'Brook,' said Lady Bedlington in low tones, when the Earl had staggered away and the Colonel sat down again, 'please be careful. If what you just said is related to the King, you may well find yourself out of favour.'

'I think I've made it plain I do not care,' said the colonel.

'Perhaps you do not, for yourself, but I hope you care for Calista's sake. After all, it was you who wanted her to be presented to the King. Are you going to spoil it for her before she even has the chance to be presented to him?'

'You are right, as always, Aunt Agatha,' said the Colonel. 'Now, let us eat lunch and forget all this unpleasantness.'

The colonel and his aunt exchanged a meaningful glance, and Calista felt, not for the first time, that she was a spectator, coming into a theatre half-way through the play.

'I do not mind if I do not meet the

King,' said Calista. 'I would much rather live in a society where a man is judged by his actions rather than by his birth.'

'Nevertheless,' said Lady Bedlington, sternly but kindly, 'you shall meet him and Brook will behave. Really, child, it is bad enough that he comes out with reactionary statements. People forgive him because he's a soldier and they're allowed to be blunt. But I fear his influence on you is a malign one and that we shall all be thrown in the tower.'

Calista laughed, because Lady Bedlington was quite clearly joking. 'I promise I will not tell the King that I did not care to meet him.'

'I'm relieved to hear it. Now if I could just extract the same promise from my great-nephew, I can attend the ball without feeling on tenterhooks.'

'I shall be the perfect gentleman,' said the Colonel. He was looking at Calista with something like admiration.

After that luncheon was a lively affair. Both the Colonel and his great aunt were tremendously witty, to the point that Calista could barely keep up with them. All she knew was that she smiled and laughed more than she had for a very long time. It was as if a dark cloud had lifted from above her head. Deep down she knew the cause of the cloud, and feared its return, but she would not think about it. Not when she felt so happy.

8

The days until the ball at St. James's Palace seemed to drag by. The Colonel was often absent, overseeing the renovations to his own home. Blanche had half a dozen invitations, insisting Evelyn accompany her, but leaving Calista behind. Not that Calista minded about that. Time without her step-sister was spent happily making the most of Lady Bedlington's library.

Both evenings, Calista and Lady Bedlington ate dinner alone, as Blanche and Evelyn had been invited elsewhere, and the Colonel and Mr. Benedict returned late from their work. Calista suspected, without proof, that Blanche was deliberately keeping Evelyn and Mr. Benedict apart.

On the morning of the ball, she looked out into the garden and saw Evelyn and Mr. Benedict talking earnestly. She could not hear what was being said, but Mr. Benedict seemed to be entreating Evelyn over something. Evelyn kept shaking her head, and trying to walk away, only for Mr. Benedict to pull her back and continue his entreaties. Finally, he drew her into his arms and kissed her passionately. Calista backed away from the window, ashamed to have been watching them at such a private moment, only to find that she met with warm, strong resistance.

'Good morning, Calista,' said the Colonel.

She spun around, and realized she was barely inches from him, but with nowhere to go. Not that she really wanted to go anywhere. 'Good morning, Colonel.' Unbidden, the image of the Colonel taking her into his arms and kissing her, as Mr. Benedict had kissed Evelyn, came to mind. 'I was just looking out to see if the weather was fair.'

'It looked rather stormy to me,' he replied.

'Do you think so? I really believe we will have sunshine.'

'Have you ever been caught in a summer storm, Calista? It can be quite exhilarating.'

Whatever they were discussing, Calista was convinced it had very little to do with the weather. 'I cannot say I that have, Colonel.'

'Mr. Benedict and Mrs. Haywood seem to be caught in one now.'

'I think,' said Calista, happy to change the subject, but still trying to eradicate the image of the Colonel kissing her from her mind, 'that he wants to be with her, but that I am holding her back.'

'Why would you do that?'

'Not deliberately,' said Calista, hastily. 'She will lose Papa's annuity if she remarries and she is afraid I won't be provided for.'

'Then we shall have to find you someone to marry, so that she can be happy.'

Her heart dropped then. How could he talk so casually about her marrying someone else? The answer was simple. He had no idea how she felt about him, and he did not feel anything for her. He had been kind to her, that was all. And she still suspected that the only reason he arranged for her to attend the St. James's ball was to get back at Blanche for the slight on his character. 'I want Evelyn to be happy,' said Calista. 'But I could not marry the Earl of Garton, not even for that.'

'The Earl?' The Colonel frowned. 'Is he still bothering you?'

'He says he wants to marry me. He has sent several notes to Lady Bedlington to that effect. And to Evelyn. I do not think he would be kind to me.'

'No, you are right to refuse. He was not kind to his late wife.' The Colonel looked at her for a long time. So long that she became lost in his eyes, and it felt as if something happened between them. Or perhaps she just imagined it had. 'I promise with my last breath, Calista, that you will marry someone who is kind to you.'

'Do I have to marry at all?' The idea of marrying anyone but the Colonel was anathema to Calista. She could not begin to imagine allowing another man to kiss and touch her, not when she loved him so dearly. 'I wondered . . . Well, the thing is, Lady Bedlington said I would always have friends and protection. I wondered if I took a job as her companion, then Evelyn would still be free from worry. I have been too shy to mention it in case she thought I was being presumptuous and that she was really only being kind. Perhaps you could suggest it to her. Or if not to your great aunt, then to some other well-born lady. I read well, I can sew and . . . '

'You most certainly will not be a paid companion.' The Colonel sounded so uncharacteristically haughty that Calista feared she had said something outrageous. 'Leave things to me. We will find a way for Harry and Mrs. Haywood to be happy and for you to be protected.'

'You promise that it won't involve marriage to the Earl of Garton or anyone like him?' Or marrying anyone else for that matter, her heart said privately. Calista did not want to hold Evelyn back, but neither did she want to spend the rest of her life married to a man she could never love. Her heart would always belong to the Colonel.

'You have my word. Shall we shake on it?' The Colonel took her hand in his without waiting for a response. For the first time neither was wearing gloves. The feel of his warm hands encompassing hers sent shockwaves through her. Instead of shaking her hand, the colonel raised it to his lips. If she had thought his touch was shockingly pleasurable, it was as nothing compared to the heat of his mouth against her bare skin. 'I will see you tonight,' he said. His grey eyes looked strangely heavy, as if he were in the grip of some emotion that Calista could not fathom.

'Yes.' How one simple word could convey so much, she did not know. She hoped that he took it at face value, and did not realize that she was saying yes to giving him her heart and her undying devotion.

The rest of the day was filled with visits and final fittings for her ball gown. Standing in front of the mirror, wearing an exquisite dress of white silk overlaid with lace, with a high waist and low neckline, Calista barely recognized the woman in the reflection. Her hair had been set in loose ringlets, piled on top of her head, and then surrounded by a thick band of silk to match her dress. Wispy ringlets framed her face.

She rushed to Evelyn's bedroom, wanting her to see the transformation. 'Evelyn?'

'What is it, dear?' Her step-mother was lying in the darkened room.

'Evelyn, are you unwell?'

'I have an upset stomach, dearest. I'm sure I will be fine soon. Oh do light the lantern and let me look at you.'

Calista did as she was bid, then approached the bed. She was horrified to see that Evelyn really did look ill. 'Perhaps I should not go tonight,' she said.

'You will go to the ball,' said Evelyn

with a wan smile. 'I would not have you miss it for the world. You look beautiful. Just beautiful.'

'Is Blanche here?'

'No, she has gone out to dine with those two sisters. I was invited too, but . . . I cannot stand their prattling when I feel well, let alone when I feel ill.'

'If you need me, you are to send for me,' said Calista. She felt guilty because as much as she cared about Evelyn's welfare, she did not want to miss the ball. Not so much because of the King, but because the Colonel would be there and she wanted him to see her new dress. If anyone had told her a few weeks before she would care what a man thought of her attire, she would have laughed at them. Now it seemed to her that everything hinged on what the Colonel thought of her tonight. She did not want to let him down in front of the King.

'He will think you are the most beautiful woman he has ever seen,' said Evelyn, perceptively.

'Do you think so?'

'Yes. I am sure of it.'

Calista rushed forward and kissed Evelyn on the forehead. 'I want you to know that if you wish to be with Mr. Benedict, then you may. You do not have to worry about me.'

'Why? Have you received an offer of marriage from the Colonel?'

'What? Oh no. Of course not. He is going to help me.'

'In what way?' Evelyn frowned. 'If he has not offered you marriage, dearest, then I hope he has not made a less reputable offer.'

'No. No, I am sure that is not what he meant. I asked him if he could find me a position as a companion to a high-born lady and he said no, but he would make sure that I was protected so that you and Mr. Benedict could be happy together.'

'Calista . . . dearest, do take care. You're a clever girl, but also very innocent in many ways. When a man offers to protect you, but does not offer marriage . . .'

Evelyn paused, leaving the rest unspoken, either out of deference for Calista's youth, or because she was too embarrassed to be more explicit. 'I am being silly, I'm sure. The Colonel has always behaved with the utmost respect towards you. But if he, or any other man for that matter, makes you any offer that involves compromising your good name, you are not to even think about my happiness. You say no, and come straight to me. Do you promise?'

'I promise.' Suddenly Calista did not feel so happy in her new dress. Had the Colonel been offering her his protection? She was not so sheltered that she did not know of the actresses and women of lower birth who enjoyed the protection of the King or other noblemen. They were spoken of in hushed tones amongst the gentry, with the gossips repeating the details in tones that managed to sound both outraged and excited at the same time.

It did not make sense. If the Colonel did not think it suitable for her to be a paid companion, he was hardly likely to offer her his protection. Was he? Men and the way their minds worked was something of a mystery to Calista. Especially men like the Colonel, who were older and much more experienced than the insipid and hesitant young men whom she met at dances in her own village. And if he was offering his protection in that way, would he really be introducing her to the king? Part of her was still concerned that his only reason for doing so was to repay Blanche for almost involving him in a duel. Perhaps Blanche had been right all along, and he was in love with her. Was it possible that he wanted to marry her step-sister, whilst keeping Calista as his mistress?

Given that Blanche had overshadowed her for so many years, it was all too easy for her to think herself into the lesser role. Blanche got what she wanted. Blanche had men lining up to dance with her, only dancing with Calista whilst they waited for her step-sister to be free. Was it possible that the Colonel only intended to amuse himself with Calista until Blanche accepted his offer of marriage?

It will not happen, she told herself silently as she went downstairs to join Lady Bedlington and the Colonel. As much as she loved him, she would not become his mistress under any terms. She would much rather starve in the gutter. If he mentioned giving her his protection again, she would tell him in no uncertain terms that she did not need it. How could she have been so naïve as to think he meant anything else by his offer?

She was halfway down the staircase before she realized he was waiting at the bottom, watching her descend. He was frowning slightly, but she barely registered that. Dressed in his uniform, with its tight-fitting red jacket, white breeches and highly polished knee-high boots, he took her breath away. Never had she seen any man look so powerful and magnificent. All her previous affirmations dissipated under a rush of desire.

It was only after she noticed the way he looked that she really took note of his frown. She wondered if he did not like what she wore. Or perhaps it was because she was not Blanche.

'You look breathtaking,' he said, his eyes watching her intently as she walked down the last few steps.

'Thank you.'

'But you also look sad, Calista. May I ask why?'

'I am not sad,' she said. It was not exactly a lie. She was not sad. Only confused, conflicted and overwhelmed with longing for him. 'I am just a little nervous about tonight. I've never seen the King before so I hope I will not do anything to disgrace myself. Or you and Lady Bedlington.'

'I am sure you will not.'

Lady Bedlington came from the salon into the hallway. She stopped and looked Calista up and down, but not in an unpleasant way. 'Oh yes, Calista. You do look charming. The King likes pretty girls, so I am sure he will take to you.

You look very handsome, Brook. Now if someone does not say something nice about my looks, I'll be inclined to sulk all evening.'

Lady Bedlington wore a gown of black satin and lace, decorated with hundreds of shiny black pearls. Calista had no idea if they were real pearls, but they were certainly spectacular. 'You look lovely,' she said.

'A picture,' said the Colonel, kissing his aunt on the cheek.

'Is the right answer.'

They travelled across London in a fine carriage, and as they drew nearer to the palace, Calista's earlier fears melted away to be replaced by abject fear. She was going to meet the King. What if he hated her? What if she did say or do the wrong thing? Exactly what did one say to the King? She knew that one did not speak unless one was spoken to. So that part should be easy. Only she had a habit, when she was nervous, of needing to fill silences. She made a mental note not to do that tonight.

They reached St. James's Palace around nine o'clock, approaching it from Pall Mall. The gate house was lit up and it was thrilling when the carriage drove through the gates. She was going to visit the Court of St. James's!

'It's hard to believe this used to be a leper hospital,' said the Colonel.

'Did it?'

'Yes, Henry the Eighth built the palace, hence the Tudor style of the architecture. Daniel Defoe considered it a bit 'low and mean' compared to other palaces in Europe.'

'I think it's a wonderful building,' said Calista. 'Defoe clearly does not appreciate good architecture.'

The carriage came to a halt inside the courtyard, which was brightly lit. Some guests were standing outside waiting for their name to be called. They waved a greeting to the Colonel and Lady Bedlington. The Colonel helped his great aunt, then Calista down from the coach. The pressure of his hand on Calista's told her that he knew just how nervous she was feeling. She hesitated slightly.

'Come,' he said gently. 'Let me present you to the King.'

Had he not been wearing all his finery, Calista might not have realized that the rather portly, out-of-breath man standing next to a matronly woman was the King. He reminded her of the grocer in her town, who always had something amusing to say whilst he packaged up the vegetables. Thinking of the King in such a light made him seem less frightening. He was after all just a man, like any other man. The years of pleasure, whilst his father refused to let him take any part in state affairs, had taken their toll, leaving George the Fourth looking like a tired, old man. The lady next to him, and his constant companion since she ousted his last mistress from his affections, was Marchioness Conyngham. It was said that the Marchioness was the only one who could deal with the King's ever-changing moods.

Calista curtseyed low, as Lady Bedlington had been teaching her for the past few days. 'Charming, charming,' said the King, smiling at Calista. 'Do we not think so, Lady Conyngham?'

'Yes, a most pretty girl.'

To Calista's great relief, the King did not say any more to her. 'Good to see you again, Colonel Windebank. Lady Bedlington. Perhaps you will join us in a game of cards later.'

'I would be delighted, Your Majesty.'

They moved further into the ante room. Through a set of double doors, Calista could see that people were already dancing.

'There,' said the Colonel, 'that was not so awful, was it?'

'No. I was afraid he would ask me something complicated and I would not be able to answer.'

The Colonel laughed and said in a low voice, 'The King would be afraid to ask anything complicated in case he did not understand the answer. Would you like some champagne?' Without waiting for a reply the Colonel stopped one of the attendants and handed a glass of champagne each to his aunt and Calista.

'One thing I like about the palace is that drinking is not forbidden,' said Lady Bedlington.

'Have you ever drunk champagne before, Calista?' asked the Colonel.

'No, but I believe I am expected to make a comment about the bubbles going up my nose.'

'I will be extremely disappointed if you do not.'

Calista took a sip of her drink, and her first thought was to wonder what all the fuss was about. The champagne was certainly not as nice as the wine they had drunk at dinner. It seemed rather heavy and gassy to her.

'An acquired taste perhaps,' said the Colonel, when she wrinkled up her nose.

'Yes, perhaps.'

She looked around to see who else was at the ball, not that she knew many people in London. She recognized a few who had attended Almacks. Everyone was dressed even more elegantly than before, but she also noticed that the atmosphere was less relaxed. One did not let one's guard down in the Court of St. James's even if there was champagne on offer.

The King was still greeting guests, and Calista almost dropped her glass when she saw that not only was he talking to the Earl of Garton but that they were looking in her direction.

9

'Shall we dance, Calista?' said the Colonel. He too seemed interested in the discussion going on at the entrance, and the frown Calista had seen on his face earlier returned.

'Yes, thank you.'

He took her hand and led her to the ballroom. The dancers were waltzing. 'I've never waltzed,' she said.

'Then let me be the first to teach you. It is not too difficult.'

It was not difficult, but it was exciting, not least because unlike most of the quadrilles and jigs that Calista had danced, the Colonel was touching her the whole time. She was acutely aware of the heat of his hands on her waist, through the thin material of her gown. Her own hand fluttered against his shoulder, almost afraid to touch him, because of the sensations he evoked in her. She knew that the waltz had been considered scandalous, and was only recently becoming popular in Britain. She could understand why. The waltz created an intimacy between a man and woman that no other dance ever had.

She felt as though she were being swept along on the air, and by the time the dance finished, she was flushed with excitement.

Another dance, a jig, started straight away.

'Shall we?' said the Colonel, his eyes looking as heavy as when he had kissed her hand earlier that day.

'Yes. Unless you would prefer to dance with one of the other ladies.'

'I would not.'

'Don't keep the girl all to yourself, Windebank,' a voice said. It was Garton. 'I wish to dance with her.'

Calista understood that to refuse would create a scene, but nevertheless she appealed to the Colonel with her eyes not to leave her with the Earl.

'Come along, Windebank.' It was the

King, and he was laughing. 'You cannot keep the prettiest girl in the room all to yourself.'

It had the manner of being a command, and one which neither Calista or the Colonel could ignore. She nodded to the Earl shyly, and they began to dance. She could only feel relief that it was not a waltz. The idea of the awful Garton touching her as the Colonel had was horrendous to her. Nevertheless she felt as if he leered over her during the times when he did have to take her hand in his.

'Need to talk to you later,' he said in staccato tones whenever they were close enough.

'I am afraid I will be attending Lady Bedlington most of the evening,' said Calista. It was a lame excuse, but the only one she could think of at the time.

'Need to talk to her too. Clear this thing up once and for all. Realise I came on a bit strong. You're young and need to be guided by a man. Will do right by you. Don't worry.'

If it was an apology, it did nothing to stem her fears. Nothing that the Earl could do would be right by Calista. It was not just her love for the Colonel that prevented her from liking him. It was a deep and abiding distaste for the Earl that had nothing to do with her feelings for any other man.

She was extremely grateful when the dance ended and another man asked her to dance. She said yes without really caring who he was. As long as he was not the Earl.

Once or twice during the next few dances, she glanced across and saw Lady Bedlington and the Earl involved in intense discussions. He would walk away, then return, seeming to berate Her Ladyship about something. The Colonel danced with a couple of other women, but he too kept looking towards where his great aunt and Garton were talking.

Eventually, and with great relief, Calista found herself dancing with the Colonel again. 'I am afraid,' she said.

They were dancing a quadrille, so there was not much chance to speak more than a few words.

'Do not be.'

The Earl of Garton had moved away from Lady Bedlington and was involved in deep discussions with the King.

'He will not take no for an answer.'

'He will have to eventually. I have told you, I will protect you.'

Calista stiffened, and almost lost where she was in the dance. Nothing more was said until it ended, at which point both she and the Colonel were summoned by the King.

Lady Bedlington was also called over.

'Now let us sort this out,' said the King. 'We are aware that Garton here is very taken with this young lady, but that she has refused him.'

Everyone stopped to listen.

'That is true,' said Lady Bedlington, when no one else spoke.

'Then it is your job to make her see sense, Lady Bedlington. We approve the match. The Earl wants the match.'

'Surely,' said the Colonel, 'Miss Haywood's own feelings on the matter should be taken into account.'

'She will be a countess. The girl would be silly to refuse. Now, Miss Haywood,' said the King. 'I realize that it is the fashion for young women to appear reluctant, but the Earl is a good catch and we approve. You are not going to disagree with your King, are you?'

'I . . . ' Calista felt as if the room swam around her. If the King were ordering her to marry the Earl and she refused, what might the consequences be? 'I do not love him.'

The King laughed. 'Such things come after marriage, child. Now, can we assume this is settled?'

'No,' said the Colonel. 'No, Your Majesty, we most certainly cannot assume it is settled.'

'You are disobeying me?' said the King.

'No, not at all, Your Majesty. You know that I trust your judgement in all things. But . . . I had not planned to announce this yet, but you have rather forced my hand.'

'Come on man, speak, speak. Announce what?'

'Miss Haywood has already agreed to become my wife. Is that not so, my love?'

The room really did spin then. Calista opened her mouth to speak then closed it again. She hardly knew how to reply. She could not denounce him as a liar in front of the entire Court, and yet she did not know how legally binding his announcement was. Did it mean they really had to get married? Or was it merely to buy time, so that Garton would lose interest? She wanted to be married to him, but he had effectively fallen on his sword for her, giving up his independence. How could she let him do that? Especially if he was not in love with her.

'Yes, that is correct,' said Lady Bedlington, when Calista did not say anything. 'It was supposed to be a secret, for now at least. My great nephew has indeed asked for and received a promise of marriage. I tried to warn him that Miss Haywood is very young and should be allowed to have her first Season in London. But what can one say when two people are so clearly in love and so clearly suited to each other?'

'Is this true, Miss Haywood?' asked the King. That was when Calista realized he was not nearly as stupid as people thought.

'Yes,' she said, somewhat breathlessly. She was lying to the King, and deep down she wondered if it were possible to be executed for such a lie. 'Yes, it is true.'

'You love the Colonel?'

'Yes.' That at least was not a lie, and judging by the King's reaction he did not doubt her words. 'Well, this calls for a celebration! Hard luck, Garton, but a promise is a promise and I am sure you would not wish these young people to renege on it.'

'I can do no more than congratulate you,' said Garton. He smiled, but his eyes were hard and cold. It sent a shiver of apprehension down Calista's spine, but that was as nothing compared to the momentous announcement the Colonel had just made to save her from marriage to the Earl. She wanted to speak to him alone, to tell him that he need not keep his promise, but it was impossible. People flocked around them, urged on by the King, wishing them luck and happiness. Some men made risqué jokes to the colonel. All the time he was watching her face. She was supposed to look happy. She knew that. And under any other circumstances, the idea of being married to the Colonel would be wonderful. Instead she felt as if her life had fallen apart.

She loved him with all her heart, but he did not love her. She was still convinced that he had only intended to offer her such protection as was offered to women of low virtue. Yet in front of the King and the entire court he had announced his intention to marry her. She had to find a way to set him free, otherwise he would spend the rest of his life resenting her.

'Well,' said Lady Bedlington as they rode back home in the early hours of the morning. 'That should give the whole of London something to talk about. You certainly know how to get everyone's attention, Brook.'

'It will be a nine-day wonder, I am sure,' said the Colonel. He was looking at Calista, who had barely been able to speak since the announcement.

'They will expect a wedding,' his great aunt said pointedly.

'And they will get a wedding.'

'So when is the happy event to take place?'

'As soon as possible. Do you not think so, Calista?'

'Surely you did not really mean it,' she said. Her throat was so constricted she could barely say the words.

'On the contrary, I meant every word. One does not announce such a thing in front of the King then change one's mind.'

'I know you only said it to be kind, so that I did not have to marry the Earl, but I am sure that if we just left it a while people would forget and . . . '

'I do not think anyone will forget. I most certainly shall not.'

'Perhaps we should talk about this tomorrow,' said Lady Bedlington. 'I think Calista is very tired, Brook, and a little overwhelmed by everything that has happened. It is not every day that a young lady meets the King and is then proposed to in court.'

'Of course,' said the Colonel. 'Forgive me, Calista. We will discuss this in the morning when you are rested.'

Calista was tempted to protest that she had not actually been proposed to. The Colonel had announced their engagement, Lady Bedlington had agreed it was already in place, and they had all lied to the King. It was not how she imagined a man would ask for her hand in marriage. And she had dreamed of the Colonel asking her to marry him. Only in her dreams they were alone and he started by declaring his love for her in the most passionate terms, taking her in his arms and telling her that he would die without her. She could see now that it had been a childish fantasy and no doubt one drawn from reading far too many silly romantic novels.

She could not escape the cold, hard reality of his so-called proposal. He had done it out of gallantry, because he knew she was afraid of being married off to the Earl. In doing so, he had betrothed himself to a woman he did not love and whom just that afternoon he had been thinking of as mistress material. A woman he could use up and throw aside when he grew bored with her.

She must speak to him and make him see sense, but it was hard to do so in front of Lady Bedlington. Surely if they both agreed the marriage could not take place, then there would be no legal implications for either of them. She could then go back to the country, away from the likes of the Earl of Garton.

They reached Lady Bedlington's town house and Calista made to go straight upstairs to bed. 'Calista, may I speak to you alone for a moment?' asked the Colonel. 'In the study?'

'You may speak to her for a few minutes and leave the study door open,' said Lady Bedlington. 'I shall be listening for Calista coming up the stairs.'

Despite her earlier wish, Calista found that she would prefer not to speak to him at that moment. Not when her emotions were so raw. But she did not feel she could refuse, so she followed him meekly into the study.

'I am sorry that the proposal was not everything that you wished for,' he said when they were alone. She put her hands to her face, to stem the blush that rose there. How could he know what she wished for?

'With all due respect, Colonel, it was not a proposal at all.'

'Yes, I realize that, and that it put you on the spot. I am still sorry it was not everything you wished for. No doubt you would have preferred to be in a pretty garden and for me to make love to you properly.'

'I . . . ' A garden had played a part in one of her fantasies. 'I do not want you to feel trapped, so if there is any way that we could . . . '

'No. I intend to marry you, Calista. So I suppose it is something we both need to get used to. This may not be the way either of us intended things to be, but one day perhaps you will come to think of our impending marriage with happiness. I am sorry it does not make you feel that way now.'

He spoke with such cold formality that Calista knew he would never say all the things she wanted him to say. Even a declaration of fondness would be better than the polite terms in which he expressed his wish that they both be happy with the arrangement. He had practically admitted that the marriage was not what he intended. His idea seemed to be that one day they would tolerate the idea. She did not want to be married to a man who only put up with her because he had nothing better to do.

'I do not understand how you can want to marry me,' she said. 'You have never said anything to make me think you see me as a suitable wife. You have never kissed me . . . you . . . ' She wanted to add 'you have never told me you love me' but she was afraid that he might say it just to please her rather than because it was true.

'Oh, so that's what's bothering you.' He smiled and moved towards her. She tried to take a step back, but he had already put his hands on her waist, pulling her to him. His mouth found hers, kissing her gently at first. She murmured and moved against him, feeling the warmth of his body through her dress and wanting to be even closer still. He responded by kissing her more passionately, bringing one of his hands up to support the back of her head as he increased the pressure of the kiss. She caressed the side of his face with her hand, fighting the compulsion to run that hand all over his body.

'Oh, Calista,' he said in husky tones when he set her lips free. His mouth gently teased her jawline. 'I think you and I will cope very well together as man and wife.'

Cope? Was that all he could offer her? A marriage where they coped? It was not what she wanted to hear. She gasped in anguish, before turning and fleeing from him, flying up the stairs to her room where she threw herself on the bed, sobbing.

10

The next few weeks passed by in a daze for Calista. She and the Colonel were invited to several functions as a couple, accompanied by Lady Bedlington as their chaperone, because Evelyn was still unwell. She had little choice but to smile and talk, when inside her heart was torn in two.

There had been no further talk of abandoning the engagement, mainly because she had no chance to be alone with the Colonel. In public, he and Lady Bedlington spoke of the marriage as though it were a fait accompli. It left Calista feeling that she was on a merry-go-round that spun faster and faster. One day, she felt sure, it would throw her off into the void.

Lady Bedlington also insisted on buying a trousseau for Calista, despite her pro-testations. 'A new bride must be dressed accordingly,' said Lady Bedlington as they waited in yet another dress shop, whilst girls modeled various dresses.

'I do not feel like a new bride,' said Calista.

'Things may not have happened as you wished, child, but they have happened,' said Lady Bedlington, kindly. 'All you can do now is make the best of them.'

'He does not love me.' It was the most honest that Calista had been so far. 'How can I marry him when he does not love me?'

'When I married my late husband it was arranged by our families. I felt much as you do. That I was some sort of marionette, being controlled by others. Then finally, after the wedding, all the strings were cut and it was just the two of us, alone together. I realized then that he was as terrified as I was and had been for just as long. I don't know if I loved him then, on our wedding day. It took some time for love to grow. I do know that when I lost him, I lost the only man I ever loved and the only man who ever loved me.'

'What if he never loves me?'

'Who said he does not?'

'He has not said he does.'

'My dear child, if you insist on waiting for a man to say the right things, then you'll be waiting forever. They never do. That is society's fault. We raise men to be stoical, not to show or express their feelings. But as you grow older you will learn to judge a man by his actions, not by his words. Then you will know without being told.'

'And what if I learn to judge him by his actions and it seems he does not love me?'

Lady Bedlington put her hand over Calista's. 'At the moment you think you are the only girl in the world beset by such fears, and that men do not worry about it, but that is not so. Whether male or female, we all want to be loved and we all fear being unloved. Even your step-sister behaves as she does out of a pressing desire to be loved and admired. Only she needs be loved and admired more than anyone else in the world. In the end that will destroy her, because she will never be able to settle for the love of one man. I do not know my great nephew's feelings for certain, as he has not confided in me. I do know from his actions that he cares about your welfare and wants to protect you from men like the Earl of Garton. Can that not be enough for you, for now?'

'I suppose it will have to be.' Calista was tempted to tell Lady Bedlington that the Colonel had offered her a very different type of protection, but she feared it would not only reflect badly on the Colonel, but also upon her. What type of girl must she seem to be to have a man make such an offer?

Lady Bedlington was right. The Colonel did care about her welfare, and was always kind and gentle with her. Even more so since they kissed. He seemed to understand her confusion and fear.

But as much as Calista tried to tell herself that it was enough that she was going to marry a man whom she trusted would never treat her unkindly, she could also see bleak years stretching ahead of her. Years in which she loved him more and more, whilst he cared for her less and less because he would rather have married someone else. The previous night she had a vivid and disturbing dream that her heart broke off one piece at a time, year by year, until eventually there was nothing more than a black hole where it used to be. What would that do to her in the long run? What kind of person would she become? She saw herself as an embittered old woman, grieving for a love she had never known, perhaps spreading poison amongst others to try and ease her own pain.

A tear rolled down her cheek. Lady Bedlington handed her a handkerchief, and whispered, not unkindly, 'Try not to cry in public, child. People expect a bride-to-be to look happy.'

When they returned to Lady Bedlington's town house, it was to find that Evelyn was once more ill in bed.

'I think it's time we called a doctor,' said Lady Bedlington. She and Calista had gone straight to Evelyn's room.

'No, it is merely a stomach complaint,' said Evelyn. 'I will be well again tomorrow. It must be something I ate.'

'That is what worries me,' said Lady Bedlington. 'Several of the servants are also ill. So it is time to get to the bottom of this. I will not have it said that I poison my guests and my staff.' She smiled and swept from the room, but Calista could see that despite Her Ladyship's witty remark, she was deeply concerned.

'Tell me, what have you bought for your trousseau today?' asked Evelyn, trying to sit up.

'Do not tire yourself.' Calista sat on the edge of the bed.

'I am so sorry I cannot come with you. I should love to see all your new clothes.'

'You will see them when they arrive. I have four new morning dresses and four new ball gowns. Though why I need so much I do not know. Unless Lady Bedlington is afraid that the Colonel will never allow me to buy another gown.'

'I do not think he will be miserly. Are you happy, Calista?'

Calista shook her head. 'Lady Bedlington says that I should be happy he is kind to me.'

'That is important. As I found out from my first husband, a man in love with you is not necessarily kind. I suppose it is because one has further to fall from the pedestal upon which they set you.'

'Oh, so you think that as the Colonel does not have very high expectations of me, he will not be as disappointed when I fail to live up to those expectations,' Calista quipped. She was relieved to see that despite all her glum moments, she still had her sense of humour.

'That is not what I meant at all, you wicked girl.' Evelyn took her hand. 'I know that this may not be all you wish it to be, darling, but I cannot tell you how relieved I am that you will be cared for, no matter what happens to me. I think . . . '

'What?'

'I have to tell someone. Blanche will not hear of it. But Mr. Benedict has been coming to see me most days. He wants to marry me.'

'Evelyn, that's wonderful!' Calista threw her arms around her step-mother's neck. 'And you said yes, of course?'

'Yes. He has worn me down. I do not think I ever stopped loving him, and there's a . . . a rightness to our getting married. Do you understand?'

'Yes, I understand.'

'It does not mean that I did not love your father.'

'Evelyn, you do not have to explain to me. I know you loved Papa, and he loved you. As he loved Mama. I am sure that our hearts are big enough to find love more than once. It is big enough to encompass our parents and our children.' As Calista spoke, she realized she had hit upon the truth in herself. Even if the Colonel never loved her, they might have children. Her heart would never be completely broken, because there would always be a part of it set aside to love her children and she would always want to do what was best for them. He would love them too. She had no doubt about that. He was not cold and uncaring like his father. Perhaps that would bring them together. And one day, he might just realize he loved her, if only as the mother of his children. It was a hope she would carry in her heart as she walked up the aisle.

'You look different,' said Evelyn. 'Resigned?'

'Yes, I think I am. But let us talk about you and Mr. Benedict. When will you marry?'

'Never!' Blanche's voice cracked like a pistol shot. Neither had realized she entered the room. 'Mama, I have told you to have nothing to do with that man.'

'And I have told you, Blanche, that I

am the mother and you are the daughter. Please, let's not argue.'

'I will not have anything standing between me and being the Duchess of Midchester.'

'I do not see how my marriage to Mr. Benedict could do such a thing.'

'He is of the lower classes.'

'He may not be a nobleman, Blanche, but he is a decent and well-bred gentleman.' Evelyn lay back on the pillow, looking exhausted. 'It is decided, Blanche, and nothing you can do will stop it.'

Before Blanche could say any more the doctor arrived. Calista and her step-sister were ushered from the room, whilst the doctor talked to Evelyn.

After he had seen Evelyn he went to call on the servants who were also sick, but would not be drawn on his conclusions immediately.

Lady Bedlington had joined Calista and Blanche in their sitting room, and the three women waited whilst the doctor made his rounds.

'I am sure Mama is perfectly well,' said Blanche. To Calista's surprise Blanche looked genuinely concerned. 'She is getting old and old people suffer from such complaints.'

'I'll have you know I have the constitution of a horse,' said Lady Bedlington. She smiled to show she was joking. Blanche sat on the sofa, wringing her hands, not seeming to listen. 'And my servants are not all old. Young Annie who tends you is only eighteen, yet she too is ill.'

'Perhaps Annie has been doing things she should not,' said Blanche.

'I doubt that very much,' said Lady Bedlington. She was no longer smiling. 'Annie is the daughter of my butler at Bedlington Hall in Midchester, and they are a good, decent family.'

'I am sure Blanche is only upset about her Mama,' said Calista.

'I do not need you to defend me, Calista.'

'Yes, you are right, Calista. I am sure your step-sister is merely concerned about Mrs. Haywood.'

'I do love Mama, you know,' Blanche said suddenly. 'Despite what people think. I love her dearly.'

'I know that, Blanche,' said Calista. She went to sit at Blanche's side.

'I do not really want her to die.'

'She is not going to die.'

'She might . . . ' Tears splashed on Blanche's cheeks. Calista could not remember if she had ever seen her step-sister cry. At least not emotional tears. Blanche was capable of angry tears, when she had tantrums, but she seemed to be genuinely distressed. 'If she had only listened to me. Now her sins have come back to haunt her, and she is being punished for them.'

'Whatever can you mean?' asked Calista. 'Evelyn is the best of women.'

'You know that is not true, Calista. Do not pretend otherwise.'

Before Calista could respond, the doctor came back into the room. His face was very serious. 'I must speak to you alone, Lady Bedlington.'

'That is not necessary,' said Her Ladyship. 'I would like to hear what you have to say in front of Miss Kirkham and Miss Haywood.' She was looking at Blanche with piercing eyes.

'It would seem,' said the doctor, 'that Mrs. Haywood and some members of your staff have been poisoned.'

'Poisoned?' Calista stared at him open-mouthed. 'But how? Who?'

'How I can answer, Miss Haywood. The symptoms suggest it was rat poison. By whom, I am afraid, I cannot answer.'

'It is a mistake, clearly,' said Blanche. 'Or perhaps one of the servants did it. Put poison in the food. I have heard of servants going mad and doing such things. You are lucky you are not dead, Lady Bedlington. No doubt one of the servants thinks you have left them a legacy, and has tried to kill us all. We are fortunate not to be afflicted.' She was speaking in feverish tones. 'But Mama will be safe now, will she not? It is not too late?' The question came out sounding as though Blanche's life depended on it.

'We will certainly investigate every-one in the household,' said Lady Bedlington. Though she spoke evenly, Calista heard a slight tremor in her voice. 'Yes, we will investigate everyone. Will they all be safe now, Doctor?'

'As long as no one ingests any more rat poison, yes. But of course, unless you know who is doing it and how it was given to them, it is hard to say.' At that moment the Colonel burst through the sitting room door.

'What is happening?' he said. 'I am told that the servants are poisoned, as is Mrs. Haywood.'

'That is correct, Brook,' said Lady Bedlington. 'It seems gossip spreads fast in this house.'

'They are all discussing it downstairs. I rushed back from my house to tell you all that . . . '

'What?' Calista saw that his grey eyes were dark and stormy. 'What has happened?'

'Mr. Benedict was set upon by some

ruffians early this morning. I found him crumpled on the doorstep. He is seriously injured. There is nowhere suitable to put him in my house, so I am having him carried up to his room here as we speak. As soon as I heard the doctor was here, I came to fetch him. Now I hear this about the poisoning. What evil is taking over here?'

'The two cannot be connected, surely,' said Lady Bedlington. No one answered her. The doctor was already following the Colonel to Mr. Benedict's room.

The next forty-eight hours were taken up with nursing all those who were sick, and the injured Mr. Benedict. Calista, Lady Bedlington and the servants who were not ill all took their turns at various sick beds. The Colonel and the male servants took care of Mr. Benedict's more personal needs.

Even Blanche helped, but only with her mother. However, for reasons of her own, Calista was reluctant to let Blanche be alone with Evelyn.

It was only after two days, when

Blanche went exhausted to her own bed, that Calista felt she could leave Evelyn for a few minutes. She needed to speak to the Colonel.

As she expected, she found him sitting at his friend's bedside. 'I need to speak to you,' she said. The colonel did not need telling twice. He followed her into Mr. Benedict's dressing room and pulled the door to.

'I am afraid,' she said, when they were alone.

'I understand that, darling. It has been a stressful few days. You should rest.'

'I am afraid it is not over, which is why I dare not leave Evelyn's side. I am also afraid to tell you what I fear. It sounds mad, even to me. Yet . . . '

'You think you are the only one who suspects what is happening here? Let me assure you that you are not.'

'There are things I cannot tell you, because they involve other people's secrets, but I think it is the key to what's happening. Only I do not want to believe that anyone could do something quite so wicked.' Her eyes filled with tears, the enormity of her suspicions too much to deal with.

'Calista.' The Colonel put his hands on her shoulders, and she immediately felt calm. His strength poured into her, and she knew things would be alright as long as he was there. She wanted to cling to him, so that she would always feel safe. 'There is nothing I do not know about Harry and Mrs. Haywood. He is my best friend and, well, men talk of such things.' The colonel lowered his voice. 'I know he is Blanche's father.'

'I think she has found out somehow and fears the truth coming out. She has said that nothing will stand in the way of her being the Duchess of Midchester. Nothing. But she could not, she would not . . . Would she?'

'I have had a man investigating Harry's assault, and it seems the ruffians were paid by someone to attack him.'

'It is too extreme,' said Calista. 'Isn't it?'

'Blanche is a woman ashamed of her

status in life. She wants it to be more than it is, believing that a rank is her right, rather than her privilege.'

'But to kill her own mother . . . Brook, it is horrifying.' It was the first time Calista had used his name. The privacy of the small dressing room seemed to invite such intimacy. He answered by taking her in his arms and kissing her. For a moment all her fears were swept away.

'I know it is frightening, darling, but it is something we must face if we are to make sure everyone is safe in the future.'

Calista rested her head on his shoulder. 'Lady Bedlington said she was afraid for you. I understand why now. I am afraid for you too. If Blanche says that nothing will stop her becoming a duchess . . .'

He laughed softly. 'As delighted as I am that you are so concerned about my welfare, I assure you I can take care of myself.'

'I would have thought Mr. Benedict

could too, but he was almost killed by those ruffians.'

'I do not stand in Blanche's way of becoming a duchess. My father's feelings for me are well known.'

'Your great aunt says that society might have other ideas.'

'My father cares less about what society thinks than I do. This is probably why he gets away with so much bad behaviour. The only way I could become the duke is by risking my father sullying my mother's good name after he is dead. I have already told you that I will not do that.'

The problem was, thought Calista, that Blanche did not know that. And she could not tell her step-sister without informing her of the Duke of Midchester's threat, which would inevitably cast a bad light on the character of Brook's mother even though the allegations were not true. She had little doubt that Blanche would take great advantage of such a slur.

Whatever else Calista did, she would

protect Brook from having his mother's name dragged through the mud. 'And still you think of protecting me,' he said, as if he had read her thought process. He stroked her cheek.

'Well why should it only be you who protects me? If we are to be married, then we should take care of each other, should we not?'

'Yes, I agree completely. And I am happy that you no longer see marriage to me as such a dreadful thing.'

'I never did. Only . . . '

'Only what?'

'It does not matter.' It did matter. It mattered very much that he did not love her as she loved him. But she liked the way they were at that moment, in each other's arms, both filled with the same sense of purpose. She would not spoil the mood by making emotional declarations that might only make him uncomfortable. 'There are more important concerns now. I have to go and . . . '

'Sleep. You have to go and sleep.

Tomorrow, when we are both rested, you and I will look into what has been happening, together.' He kissed her again, before saying huskily, 'Go to bed woman, before I forget I am a gentleman.'

11

'I wonder if I've got it terribly wrong,' said Calista. She and the Colonel had met in the study, to discuss the events of the past few days. 'Blanche seems genuinely concerned for Evelyn. Normally I would suspect her of pretending, but I have seen her cry real tears.'

'Perhaps she is a better actress than you realize,' said the Colonel. 'We must get to the bottom of this, before anyone else is hurt.'

'Yes, of course. What is happening about the men who attacked poor Mr. Benedict?'

'My agents have not yet found out who paid the ruffians to attack him, but we will get answers, I am sure.'

'I cannot imagine how Blanche would even know how to employ such men. She never goes out alone, and whilst I do not know much about it, I assume that the men were from the rougher part of London. There is no way Blanche would venture to such a place on her own. She values herself rather too much for that.'

'Then she is not working alone.'

Calista was astonished. 'You think she has inveigled someone else into this awful plot?'

'If, as we suspect, she has managed to poison her Mama and the servants, then she would need someone to get hold of the poison for her. Just as she would not go to the rougher areas of London, I cannot imagine she would go into a pharmacy and ask for rat poison. Assuming that is what was used. In fact,' said the Colonel thoughtfully, 'I think it is in fitting with Blanche's nature to get someone else to do the dirty work for her.'

'Yes, you are probably correct in that assumption.'

'First we need to find out what was used to poison Mrs. Haywood and the servants, then we can make investigations. We will visit all the pharmacies in the area and ask who they have sold the poison to recently.'

'We? You mean I may come with you?' Calista felt her heart lift.

'Unless you would find it distressing.'

'Oh no. I mean, yes, it is distressing to see how Evelyn and the servants suffer, but I cannot deny it would be exciting to help you investigate. Is that awful of me?'

'No, not at all. When I was in the army I often had to investigate wrong-doing by my men. Even in the most awful circumstances, I found myself excited by the thrill of the chase. You have a quick mind, Calista. I think you will be a great help to me.'

He could not have paid her a better compliment if he had said she was beautiful.

'But first,' he continued, 'we must find out how the poison was adminis-tered.'

'I keep feeling that I am missing something,' said Calista. 'Something important happened, only it did not seem important at the time. It was one of those trivial everyday events that . . . ' She paced the room. 'So much for my quick mind,' she said with a wry smile.

'That's only because you're thinking too hard at the moment. Let us go for a drive in the phaeton, and talk of other things. Then perhaps it will come to you.'

'I am afraid to leave Evelyn alone with Blanche for too long.'

'Blanche has gone out this morning to visit some friends. Aunt Agatha arranged it at my behest. I thought it might be a good idea to get her out of the way for a while. We have plenty of time, and I gather Mrs. Haywood is much improved this morning, as are the servants.'

'Yes, Evelyn was certainly more cheerful this morning. How is Mr. Benedict?'

'Improved, but still in a bad way. I've left my valet caring for him.'

Calista and the Colonel took a leisurely drive in the phaeton, and she could not help but notice how handsome he looked with his hands on the reins. Judging by the admiring looks he drew from female pedestrians, she was not the only one who thought so. She could still only marvel that she was to marry him, and was convinced that he would be snatched away from her at the last minute. He might meet another young woman that he fell in love with. She had to find a way to let him know that he was free to do so, even though the thought of it was like an arrow to her heart. His kisses of the night before told her that he was attracted to her, but her memory reminded her that he had only meant to offer her his protection. Not his hand in marriage, and not his love.

She, however, would love him for the rest of her life. She had managed to convince herself that their marriage could work, especially if they had children, but deep down she ached for the love he would never give her.

'How is your house coming along?' she asked, trying to free herself from the painful thoughts.

'Things have slowed down a little, due to Harry being out of action, but he left detailed plans, and the builders are good men who know how to follow them. It might not be finished as quickly as I hoped. I wanted it completed by our wedding day. That may not happen now.'

'Colonel . . . '

'Do you not think that as we are to be married you should call me Brook? Otherwise I shall feel like I'm your commanding officer, rather than your husband.'

'Is that not the same thing?' Calista said, smiling and showing her dimples.

He smiled back. 'I hope you will not think so, Calista. I hope that you will always look upon us as equals.'

'What I wanted to say . . . Brook . . . is that if you met someone else before we married, I would not hold you back. I want more than anything else for you to be happy.'

'And you think we will not be happy together?'

'I . . . I suppose that I have always believed a man and woman should be in love when they marry. I know it is naïve of me but . . . '

'Well then I suppose I should make you the same promise. That if you meet someone else, I will set you free. Only . . . ' He frowned. 'Only I will not. If I even think of you liking another man more than you like me, I will call the blighter out. Whatever you may feel now, Calista, this marriage will happen. I did not put my reputation on the line in front of the King for it to be otherwise.'

'But this is what I am trying to say. You should not feel you have to marry me out of duty, either to me or the King. I . . . '

'Enough! I do not like the turn this conversation has taken. We are supposed to be working together to help find out if Blanche has poisoned her mother and half of my great aunt's household, and you seem intent on tearing us apart.'

'No, that is not it. I . . . ' Calista seldom pouted but she did at that moment. 'So we are to be equals until you decide you do not like the way a conversation is turning. Then you call 'enough' and suddenly you are the commanding officer again. I can only obey.'

'If that is what it takes to get you up the aisle so that neither of us looks a fool, yes.' She heard him take in a deep breath. 'I am sorry I am not what you wished for in a husband, Calista. But I promise you that I will treat you well and I will not resort to commanding you. Once we are married. Until then, I am not taking any chances.'

How could he think that he was not everything she wished for? She had dreamed of meeting a man like him, only to find that when she did meet him, he was even better than the dream. Because he was not only incredibly handsome and clever, he was human and flawed. He moved from being the nebulous image of her fantasies to being a real, warm-bodied, human being who drove her almost insane with his kisses. It was only because she knew he did not love her that she found it impossible to tell him of her feelings. It would only make him feel awkward, and might also mean that if he did meet someone else, he would feel duty-bound to stay with her out of some sense of honour. Yet her love was there, demanding to be heard, to the point that she was afraid she might one day explode and ruin everything.

'We are getting off the subject in hand,' she said eventually. They were driving through Hyde Park. Walkers and riders were enjoying the early spring sunshine, and she wished she could do the same. She should enjoy being in a magnificent phaeton with a magnificent man, but it only served to remind her that she was not worthy of his love. Only his protection.

'That was the point of coming out,' he replied. 'To take our minds off the case. So to speak. But I did not intend us to argue, Calista. Nor did I intend to dominate you.' He took another deep breath. 'Of course, if you should meet and fall in love with someone else, I would not stand in your way. I want you to be happy too, and if you cannot be that with me, then I suppose I must accept you will find happiness with someone else.' His lips set in a thin line and he tightened his grip on the reins to the extent that his knuckles turned white.

Never, she thought secretly. She would never be happy with anyone else. She had made him angry and did not know how to put things right. 'Perhaps we should go back,' she suggested, 'since this is not working. Surely the scene of the crime is the best place to be to pick up clues.'

'Yes, perhaps you are right. It is nearly time for luncheon anyway.'

He turned the horses expertly and they drove back to Lady Bedlington's. She was in the hall when they arrived, talking to one of the servants. 'Good news,' she said to Calista and the Colonel. 'The servants have made a complete recovery. I have given them all a few days off so that they are fully rested.'

'And my step-mother?' asked Calista.

'She does very well, is that not right?' Lady Bedlington turned to the servant she had been speaking to.

'Yes, M'lady. She is out of bed and sitting in a chair. Miss Blanche has just taken her some tea and honey.'

'Honey!' Calista exclaimed. 'Oh, it was the honey!' She dashed up the stairs, closely followed by the colonel. When she reached Evelyn's bedroom, she was just in time to see Blanche hand her mother a cup of tea. 'Stop it!' she cried, rushing forward and knocking the cup out of Blanche's hand. It shattered on the floor.

'What on earth are you doing, Calista?'

'You poisoned the honey. That's why your mother and the servants are ill. They all had some.'

'Poisoned? How ridiculous.' Despite

her words, Blanche's eyes were watchful. 'Why on earth would I do such a thing?'

'Somehow you found out the truth about your mother and Mr. Benedict. About your illegitimacy. So you thought to poison your mother and have Mr. Benedict killed so that their secret died with them.'

Blanche knelt at her mother's feet. 'Mama, tell them the truth. Tell them how sorry I was when I realized what I had nearly done?'

'Blanche overheard us talking, Calista, when I told you about it. She was frightened for her future.'

Calista looked at her step-mother, aghast. 'You knew?'

'I guessed, yes,' said Evelyn. 'But Blanche knows she did wrong. She is truly sorry.'

'But you nearly died. The servants nearly died.'

'But we did not die,' said Evelyn. 'We cannot have a scandal. You do understand that, don't you, Calista? It would not only ruin Blanche but everyone in this house. Is that not right, Colonel?'

'No, it cannot be so,' said Calista.

'Your step-mother is right,' said the Colonel. His lips were set in a grim line. 'I understand how you feel, Calista. But such a scandal would bring shame upon my aunt's family name and mine.'

'So you're just going to let things be? Let her get away with attempted murder?'

'I have seen the error of my ways,' said Blanche. 'Despite what you think, Calista, there was no poison in that cup you just knocked from my hands. You may have it tested if you want. All I have wanted for the past few days is for Mama to recover. I did not realize how much I loved her until I nearly lost her.'

Despite Calista's misgivings, she believed everything Blanche had just said. Blanche had learned her lesson, at least where danger to Evelyn was concerned. But not only Evelyn had been harmed. Mr. Benedict was still unwell, and whilst the servants had recovered, things might have gone very differently. Then there was the niggling doubt in Calista's mind as to why the Colonel was so keen to let Blanche get away with it. Was he protecting her because he was in love with her, as Calista had suspected all along?

'I suppose then that I must go with the majority view,' said Calista. She felt let down. By Evelyn, and by the colonel. Whilst she could understand why the highwayman had turned to crime, she could not condone the same behaviour in Blanche. Certainly not just for the sake of a grand title. She realized that it was perhaps a fault within her. That she despised her step-sister so much that she wanted to see her punished. It was a feeling of which she was not very proud, but it was there and would not go away.

'We will discuss it later,' said the Colonel. She was aware of his eyes searching her face.

'There is nothing to discuss, since everything has been decided.'

'Calista, dearest, Blanche is my daughter and despite her wrongdoing I love her. This is, after all, partly my fault.'

'She just hates me and wants me to die,' said Blanche. That was the manipulative Blanche that Calista knew and despised. The one who turned everything to her benefit, even Calista's misgivings about her escaping the consequences of her actions.

'I am sure that is not true,' said the Colonel. 'None of us want you to die, Blanche. Calista?'

'No, of course I do not want Blanche to die. I . . . I need some time alone.' She fled the room in tears, churned up by all her conflicted emotions.

Calista normally laughed at young women who used headaches as an excuse to hide away from the world, but for the rest of the day she did just that. She refused to join the others for lunch, and then again at dinner time. It seemed to her that the world was upside down when someone who had almost murdered half a dozen people could simply get away with it just to avoid a scandal. She recognized her own dislike and jealousy of

Blanche played a big part in her feelings, but that did not mean that her step-sister deserved to escape justice.

She was just about to undress and get into bed when there was a knock on the door. It was Lady Bedlington.

'I am sorry I have not been down to dinner,' said Calista.

'You're unhappy, child, I can see that.' Lady Bedlington closed the door behind her and took Calista's hands. 'I am not happy with the way things turned out either. Like you I feel that justice should be served. But unfortunately Brook and Mrs. Haywood are correct. If this got out, the scandal would affect us all.'

'I do not understand why it should reflect badly upon the innocent,' said Calista.

'Oh but it does, dear girl. You are very young and idealistic, and very special for being that way. But I have lived in this world for longer. I have seen these scandals come and go, and the effect they have upon those who were innocent. Society tends to judge a family as a whole being, rather than by its individual members. That is why Blanche will not be brought to trial, and why Brook will never try for his father's title. He is not just thinking of his mother's good name, but the good name of all our family.'

'How can we ever trust her again?' asked Calista. 'How can Evelyn even dare to take a drink of tea from her?'

'It is hard to understand it, but I do believe that Blanche is truly sorry for almost killing her mother. However . . . ' Lady Bedlington paused. 'That is not to say that she will not do something else stupid to someone that she does not love so well. We must be on our guard, you and I.'

'Oh, and what if she does?' said Calista. 'It would only be hushed up again for the good of the family and . . . ' She stopped. 'I am sorry, Lady Bedlington. I spoke out of turn. I did not mean to sound so angry with you.'

'I know, dear. And I understand exactly what you are saying. But we must cross that bridge if and when we come to it.' Lady Bedlington turned to leave then said, 'Are you sure that Blanche's attempt at murder is the only reason you wish her to be punished?'

'No,' said Calista, shame-faced. 'No, probably not.'

'Well, I understand that too. But you are a good girl, Calista, and the fact that you have admitted it shows that you do not really wish her to be punished for anything other than what she has done to her mother, Mr. Benedict and the servants.'

'I wish I could be sure that was true,' said Calista. 'But . . . '

'Yes, what is it?'

'Mr. Benedict. There is no way Blanche could have arranged that. She must have been working with someone.'

Lady Bedlington nodded. 'Yes, Brook said as much. But Blanche refuses to name anyone else.'

'I think I know who it is,' said Calista.

12

The days passed by until Calista woke up one morning and realized it was her wedding day. She had barely seen the Colonel since Blanche's plot was revealed. He and Mr. Benedict, who had made a full recovery, were out most of the day, only returning late in the evening after dinner. There was no chance for Calista to be alone with the Colonel. She had so many fears and doubts, but she knew that the right words from him, even if they were not 'I love you', would make all the doubts go away.

'You look lovely,' said Evelyn, after she had helped Calista into her wedding gown. It was white satin with an intricate lace design on the bodice. A whisper-thin veil covered her head.

'Thank you.'

'Calista, dearest, we have not had much chance to talk since . . . well since everything happened. I know you are disappointed in me . . . '

'No, I am not, Evelyn. I understand that it is your duty to protect your child.'

'And yet in doing so, I have lost you. I can feel it.'

'I am not your child.' It was a simple statement of fact, so Calista was surprised to see the hurt in Evelyn's eyes. Since the events of which Evelyn spoke, Calista had felt increasingly isolated. She began to wonder who would stick up for her if she ever did anything wrong. She had no mother or father of her own, and whilst Lady Bedlington was always kind to her, she was not a blood relation and would always put the family name first. As for the Colonel . . . his dismissal of Blanche's wrongdoing for the sake of avoiding a scandal hurt more than anyone else's. And yet in a few hours' time she would be his wife. How could she bear it? If only her feelings for the Colonel and hatred of Blanche were not so closely combined by her certainty that he had other reasons for protecting her step-sister.

'You may not believe this, Calista, but I would have done the same for you.'

'I would not have tried to poison you.'

'Please do not do this, darling. Do not push everyone away because you are angry with us. Because you do not think we did the right thing. It was as much for you as for anyone. You do not want your marriage to the Colonel marred by scandal right from the beginning. Society can be very cruel.'

'The colonel assured me that he did not care for what society thinks. I suppose he only thought so when there was no danger of it happening, due to his war record. In the end it turns out he is just like everyone else, terrified of losing his place in it.'

'Calista! This is no way to talk of the man you are going to marry.'

'Oh why not, Evelyn? He is not marrying me because he loves me. He is marrying me because he was cornered into it at St James Palace. You as much as said yourself that he only intended to offer me his protection. And it is I who must live with that reality. Not society.'

'I . . . ' Evelyn looked helpless. 'I may have been wrong.'

'It is more likely that you were right. Honestly I do not understand why he did not just ask Blanche to marry him if she is what he wanted.'

Evelyn took Calista's hand. 'I do not say this to be unkind, darling. You are clearly unhappy enough as it is and I have no wish to add to that. But for a clever girl you can be very obtuse at times.'

Before Calista could ask Evelyn what she meant, a servant arrived to let them know that the carriage was waiting to take them to the church. As Calista had no male relative to give her away, Mr. Benedict had agreed to do it. The Colonel had asked one of his fellow officers to stand in as best man. He was waiting for them in the hall.

'You look very beautiful, Miss Haywood,' he said kindly. He was one of the few people Calista was not angry with. She knew from things that had been said that hiding the scandal had cost him almost as much as it had cost her. She sensed there was an estrangement between Mr. Benedict and Evelyn and was genuinely sorry for it. She still loved her step-mother and did want her to be happy with the man she loved. It seemed that Blanche had succeeded in destroying any hopes of that.

She tried to swallow some of her own self-pity. At least she was marrying the man she loved, even if he did not feel the same way. Perhaps all she felt was nerves because it was her wedding day and that all the tense feelings would disappear as soon as she was married. But there was something else too. Something at the back of her mind that told her the troubles were not over yet. What form they might take, she did not know. Only that as she climbed into the carriage on a bright sunny day, a cloud crossed the sun and the light became dark. She shivered involuntarily.

'Are you cold, Miss Haywood?' asked Mr. Benedict. The carriage set off towards the church.

'No, I am well, thank you.'

'Nervous?'

'Yes. A little. Very.' She smiled.

'You are marrying a good man today. Let me take this chance to wish you both all the happiness in the world.'

'Thank you.' Calista struggled to smile, feeling more like crying. 'I hope . . . I hope you and Evelyn shall be happy one day too. If it is not presumptuous for me to say so.'

'Thank you . . . Calista. I know that you and I share the same opinion about recent events. I have tried to follow Evelyn's wishes, but . . . I had always thought that when I had a child I should love it unconditionally. It is difficult to find out one not only has a child, but that it is impossible to even like that child. I have to remind myself that Evelyn has had to live with our mistake, and has suffered for it. She cannot turn her back on Blanche now. And in many ways it is our fault the way Blanche turned out. We were reckless when we were young. No, I was reckless. I cannot bring myself to blame Evelyn. I gave no thought to the consequences of my actions. Now we are both paying for our youthful transgressions. Even if society does not punish, God finds a way.'

Calista did not know what to think of a God who could bring so much unhappiness on two people who were genuinely in love. 'Evelyn still loves you. I know that much, and I do so want you both to be happy.'

'It is odd the way life works out. Your mother and father are blessed with Portia. Myself and Evelyn somehow give rise to Lady Macbeth.'

Calista laughed for the first time in many days, albeit in a bittersweet way. 'I am sorry, I should not laugh.'

'Yes, you should, for that was my

intention. I know you are very confused and conflicted by the things that have happened, added to the nervousness that all new brides feel. But I promise you that by the end of today, all your worries will be eradicated. You will be happy with Brook, Calista. I guarantee it.'

'And you and Evelyn?'

'We will work our way through things I am sure. But we are not your concern. You must concentrate on your own life from now on.'

Calista shyly reached out and took Mr. Benedict's hand. 'Thank you for agreeing to give me away today. I cannot think of anyone else whom I would prefer to do it.'

'And I am very proud to have been asked to escort such a beautiful bride on her wedding day.'

The church was full of people that Calista barely knew. Only Evelyn, Lady Bedlington and Blanche were familiar faces in the crowd. It once again illustrated how isolated she was. Soon,

215

she thought, as she walked up the aisle, she would be married to a man who had no love for her. She hesitated slightly, almost losing her footing, before raising her chin and deciding to meet whatever came afterwards head on. She was not a coward, and she did love the Colonel. Whether it would be enough to make her happy, she did not know. All she did know, as she saw him waiting at the altar, dressed in his uniform and with a fellow officer at his side, was that she wanted to be married to him.

Mr. Benedict went through the formalities of giving her away, her hand trembling as he put it into the Colonel's. She assumed that she made all the right responses to the officiating vicar, but afterwards, when they were pronounced man and wife, she had little recollection of having done so. She was, however, very aware of the Colonel's voice repeating the vows. It resonated throughout the church, and she imagined she must sound very mouse-like in comparison.

'You may kiss the bride,' said the

vicar. The Colonel . . . her husband . . . lifted her veil. She expected a peck on the cheek so she was unprepared for the emotions that assaulted her when he took her in his arms and kissed her full on the lips. The kiss was wonderful and devastating at the same time. Wonderful, because his kisses always were, but devastating because she was convinced it was either for show or to make Blanche jealous. Or perhaps even a little of both.

As the kiss went on and on, she could hear the congregation somewhere in the background. Some were saying 'aw' and others were laughing uncomfortably. The British were not used to such obvious shows of affection, especially in public.

She did not know who broke the spell, she or Brook, but she was grateful that even when he took his lips from hers he still held her around the waist as she was sure she might stagger backwards.

'My wife at last,' he whispered.

The next few hours passed by in a daze, with Calista feeling like a puppet whose strings were being controlled by other people. She merely went where she was told, and spoke when she was spoken to.

The wedding party returned to Lady Bedlington's where a wedding breakfast had been laid on. There were several speeches. Some, by Brook's brother officers, jokingly alluded to the coming night, only just staying on the right side of decency. No one seemed to mind. Even Lady Bedlington laughed, despite blushing in a very old lady-like manner. If Lady Bedlington's cheeks were pink, Calista imagined her own to be scarlet. She had almost managed to push the thought of sharing a bed with Brook to the back of her mind, apart from the fevered dreams over which she had no control.

Soon it was time for Calista to change into her going away outfit. They were to spend a night at Brook's house, before leaving for their honeymoon the next day. Calista had no idea where they were going. Brook had not shared the information with her. It was another indication of her lack of control over her own life. She wondered if she would always feel this way.

'Thank God that's all over,' said Brook, as they drove back to his house in the carriage. It was on Calista's lips to snap that she was sorry marrying her had proved such an ordeal, but she clamped her mouth shut. He had no choice but to marry her, after the King had forced his hand by trying to betroth Calista to the Earl of Garton. 'Now we'll have chance to talk,' he said, softly. 'I've arranged that once dinner is served the servants will have the evening off so we can be alone.'

'That will be . . . nice . . . '

'Nice?'

'I mean good, that we can talk at last. Because I've been thinking . . . We don't have to . . . what I mean is . . . as far as everyone is concerned, we are married now. So no one else will know what happens inside our marriage. So if you want to . . . to see other ladies . . . ' Her voice caught in her throat. 'I shan't stop you. I'm sure you'll find them far more interesting than me and . . . Well we hardly need bother each other at all, do we?'

'Bother each other?'

She wished he would stop responding with a question. Especially questions that insisted she be specific about what she meant.

'Are you saying that you do not wish to share my bed?'

'No . . . I mean . . . well only if you would rather not. If there is someone else you prefer . . . '

Brook frowned. 'I am willing to put your reluctance down to shyness, rather than be offended by it.'

'I am sorry, I did not mean to offend you.'

'Very well, Calista. I shan't bother you tonight, if that's what you prefer. But you do understand that if we are to have children . . . which is something I would very much like . . . then we will have to . . . bother each other, as you so quaintly put it, sometimes. Do you understand that? Has your step-mother spoken to you about tonight?'

'Oh yes. We had an excruciating conversation about it last night. I am not sure who was more embarrassed, Evelyn or me.'

'I can imagine.' Brook smiled, and it reminded Calista why she had fallen in love with him. Of course she wanted to share his bed and have his children. How could she have been so stupid as to suggest otherwise? Only she did not know how to retract her statement without looking even more stupid than she already did. He became more serious. 'I am rather hurt that you would foist me off on another woman, Calista. I had hoped . . . ' He sighed. 'Never mind what I hoped. I can see now I've been a fool. There will be no other women for me, and there will most certainly be no other men for you.'

'I would never . . . ' Calista's face felt

as if it was on fire and she glanced at him in horror. 'I did not mean that I would want to see other men. I am not like that.'

'Yet you think I am the sort of man who would take a mistress? You are allowed to feel offended by such an insult, but I am not. Is that it?'

'No. No, of course not. Oh nothing I say is coming out right. I only wanted you not to feel trapped, that is all. I know you only married me to save me from the Earl of Garton and because you promised the King you would, and that there is someone else you prefer, but . . . '

The carriage lurched to a halt outside Brook's house, preventing her from saying anything else. What a mess she had made of things. Why was it so difficult for her to say to him 'I love you, and I hate that you do not love me'? She put it down to the lack of control she had been feeling for quite some time. If she admitted she loved him, without his returning that affection, then he might have even more control over her. He might even use her love against her as a means of making sure he always got his own way. He was a man used to having his demands obeyed. She could not take the risk of being just another soldier under his command. She had to keep something of her own, even if it was only the secret of her love for him.

'I think you have said more than enough,' he muttered as he helped her down from the carriage. The servants were coming from the house to welcome them home. 'So tonight at dinner I will talk and you will listen.'

'I am not one of your soldiers to command,' she hissed, with one last attempt at liberty. It fooled no one, certainly not him. His grip on her waist as he led her up the steps to the house told her exactly who was in charge.

She had little time to take in that the renovations to the house had been completed, and that the outside looked far less derelict than it had before. She was only aware of a loud crack, then

Brook stumbling against her, almost knocking her off balance. She thought at first that he had tripped on the step, until she saw blood running from his temple. She caught him in her arms, and they both slipped, landing with a thud on the top step, her arms held tightly around him. 'Brook . . . ' Her voice was barely above a whisper, until the full horror of what had happened finally dawned on her. Only then did she scream his name.

13

A shaft of sunlight broke through a gap in the curtains, casting a glow on the bed where Brook lay with his head bandaged. Several days had passed by, in which Calista refused to leave his side. She lay on top of the bed, fully dressed, with her hand on his chest, feeling the rise and fall of his laboured breathing

'I am afraid, Mrs Windebank,' said the doctor, on the first day, 'all we can do now is wait. I have retrieved the bullet from the Colonel's head, but it is uncertain how much damage it may have done. His body may well heal itself or . . . '

'Or what? Please do not try to spare me the details, doctor. I need to know.'

'He may suffer amnesia. That is the best we can hope with such an injury. Or he may well be in a vegetative state for the rest of his life. If that is the case, then it is perhaps best that he does not live too long.'

She had asked the doctor not to spare her the details, but she could have done without that last bit of information. That someone so vibrant and healthy may spend the rest of his life unconscious was too much to bear. She knew that it happened. A girl from her town had fallen from her horse, striking her head on a rock, and was sent to a home for the mentally ill because her parents could not cope with her at home. Calista could not even think of sending Brook to such a place.

'Please wake up and be well,' she said softly as she lay by Brook's side. 'I have so much I need to tell you. If you cannot wake up, please don't be in any pain.' She reached for his hand, hoping, as she had hoped for several days, that he might respond by squeezing her fingers. 'What can I do to help you?'

There was a faint knock at the door, and one of the servants came in. 'The

Duke of Midchester is downstairs and wishes to see his son, Mrs. Windebank.'

'Of course,' said Calista. 'Give me a moment to make myself presentable, then show him up.' Perhaps Brook's father would be able to help. He might even know of a physician who could undo the damage that had been done. She went to the mirror and straightened her hair as best she could, and then adjusted her old grey muslin dress which had ridden up a little. She wore it because none of the fine clothes in her trousseau seemed appropriate for tending Brook. She still looked untidy to her own eyes, but guessed that the Duke of Midchester would not be interested in her anyway.

'Your Grace,' she said, curtseying as the duke entered the room.

'You are my son's wife?' He barked out the question, without bothering to return her greeting.

'That is correct.'

'But I gather that the marriage is not fully legal.'

'I am not sure what you mean.'

'It can be annulled.'

'Annulled? Why?'

The duke made his meaning clear in terms that embarrassed Calista greatly. 'I see. Yes, I suppose that is true, but . . . '

'But nothing. You are to go away from here and let me and people who are more suitable care for my son.'

'Go away?'

'That is what I said. Are you an imbecile? No, you cannot be. I gather you were clever enough to ensnare my son, using the King to get to him.'

'That is not true,' said Calista. 'I had no thoughts of marrying Brook until the Earl of Garton tried to force my hand.'

'So you admit it is not a love match?'

'I admit nothing of the sort.'

'Look girly, I'll give you a lot of money to leave. You are not a suitable wife for the future Duke of Midchester. You must see that. And he can hardly be a husband to you in this state. You're young enough to start again. Leave my son to me.'

'You mean the son that you have neglected for thirty years?'

'Do not take that tone with me, Miss.'

'Mrs. I am Mrs. Windebank. I am not the wife of the future Duke of Midchester. I am the wife of Colonel Brook Windebank, and I would never leave him to you. You have shown no sign of caring for him before. Why the sudden interest now?'

'He is my son. Regardless of what I might have said in the past, or what people might believe, he will be the next duke. And as I have already said, you are not a suitable wife for him. Look at the state of you. Your hair is a mess, and that dress is not fit for a servant.'

'Well I apologise for not meeting your exacting standards, Your Grace, but might I remind you that I have been at your son's side for two days, caring for him. Where have you been?'

'Trying to track down the rogue who

tried to kill him.'

'Oh . . . Then I am sorry. But the matter still stands. I will not leave him to you. You may have a hankering to care for him now, because his life has been in danger, but what happens when you tire of that? Who will take care of him then? Or will you leave him to the care of servants?'

'There are hospitals . . . '

'No! Never.' Calista was immediately reminded of the tragic girl from her home town. 'I will not let him go to one of those places.'

'I am his father.'

'And I am his wife.'

'And you fancy being the Duchess of Midchester no doubt.'

'I do not care *that* — ' Calista snapped her fingers. ' — for being the Duchess of Midchester. You may not think that our marriage is a love match, and perhaps Brook does not love me. But I love him . . . ' Tears splashed from her eyes. 'And I'll care for him here for as long as I have to.'

'Do not make an enemy of me, Missy.'

'No, Your Grace, it is you who should not make an enemy of me. When it comes to my husband, I promise I will fight you tooth and nail in order to do what is best for him.'

'Oh you silly girl . . . ' The Duke sighed, and suddenly looked very old. 'I do believe you love him. Can you be sure that your love will last any longer than what you call my sudden interest in him?' He sat down on a chair near to the window, and pulled back the curtain to look out.

'I am far more constant than you, Your Grace.'

'You think so? Then it might surprise you to hear that I loved my wife. I loved her until the day she died. Only . . . I was a young fool when we married, and had no idea how to show my love. I had not much experience of it from my own parents who despised each other for all their married life together. So I treated her as cruelly as my father treated my mother because I knew no other way. I am not proud of myself but sometimes when one has taken a road in one's life it is hard to turn back, to admit one is wrong. Then . . . ' The duke laughed bitterly, and gestured to the bed. 'Then this young whippersnapper came along and challenged me to a duel. All I wanted was my wife's love and my son's love, yet I had taught them both to hate me. So it was easier to hate in return.'

'He does not hate you. He came to you wanting you to recognize him as your son.'

'So, I got it wrong again. And I suppose I have got you all wrong too.'

'We could care for him together,' said Calista. 'I do not think I can do it all on my own. But not in a hospital. It must be here, in his home. In our home.'

'Now why would you want an old brute like me around my son?'

'Because you have just told me that you love him. I believe that when you came here today, as clumsily as you behaved, it was also because you love him.'

'Clumsily, hey? Not many people in my life have ever spoken to me as you do.'

'You had better get used to it, Your Grace, when it comes to your son's well-being.'

'When I walked in this room I thought you were the worst possible wife for a man like my son. You're young . . . far too young . . . and you look as if one gust of wind would blow you right over. Yet you have a spine as solid as any oak tree that has withstood a thousand storms. I can see that now. I do not suppose you would share some luncheon with a clumsy old man? Tell me all about my son. I know so little of him, you see.'

'I would be delighted to.'

Luncheon was a strange affair. They ate in the small sitting room off Brook's bedroom, because Calista would not go far from him. The duke showed every sign of being irascible for the rest of his life, but he also showed signs of trying to be a different man. They almost argued several times, as they disagreed about the best care for Brook, and at one point the duke threw down his napkin and looked as if he were about to leave. But he took a deep breath and stayed. The sudden deep breath was a characteristic Calista had noticed in Brook, and she wondered how much of his father's temper he had, but suppressed. It must have taken a lot of self-control to not give in to the darker forces in his nature, because he was determined not to be his father. But he had also suffered a serious head injury. Even if he awoke, might it change him, releasing those darker forces? It was something she would worry about if and when he awoke. The important thing was that he did wake up.

The duke stayed for the rest of the afternoon, watching over his son whilst Calista slept for a few hours. Not that she slept well. She kept waking suddenly, certain that she had heard Brook's voice cry out.

'You did not tell me what happened

with your investigation,' Calista said to the duke as he was leaving. 'Do you know who shot Brook?'

'I have an idea. And I am afraid it is my fault, Calista. May I call you Calista?'

'Yes, you may.'

'It was young Purbeck, I believe. He has fled to the continent and I doubt he shall return. I have played games with too many young men just like him, letting them believe they have a chance of being named my heir whilst I have them dancing around me, doing my bidding. Most get bored of being my puppets and move on. It is fair to say that they are not always the most intelligent of young men, and have no real idea of the laws of primogeniture. Purbeck really believed I intended to name him as my heir. No doubt aided by your step-sister, who had her eye on being the duchess.'

'She could have been,' said Calista. 'I think Brook . . . I think he cares for her.'

'Then you are a bigger fool than I thought.' The duke did not speak unkindly. 'And if you are right and my son cares for her and not you, then he is also a bigger fool than I thought.'

'I do believe that was a compliment, Your Grace.' Calista smiled.

'Treasure it. I shall not make many more.' The duke smiled too. It was clear he was not used to it as the smile dropped almost immediately. 'Thank you for giving an old man a second chance. I only hope that if my son awakes, he will do the same.'

'I will be your strongest champion, Your Grace.'

'I do not deserve that, but thank you again.'

Calista bid him farewell, then went back upstairs. She lay down on the bed next to Brook, as she had done so since he was carried there. She reached her hand out and put it on his chest and wondered if she only imagined that his breathing seemed a little easier. She almost jumped out of her skin when he suddenly turned to face her, his grey eyes piercing into her.

'Brook! You're awake.' She would have sat up, but his arm moved across her body and pinned her down. 'Do you know who I am?'

'Yes, you're Boadicea.'

Her heart dropped. He had lost his memory. 'No, I am Calista. Your . . . wife.'

'Strange. In the dream I had earlier, you were definitely Boadicea, charging at my father, before thwarting him and turning him into a very willing slave. Tell me, who are you and what have you done with my timid little wife?'

'Your father was here.'

'I know. I heard you talking to him. I was awake all the time he sat with me too, but I wanted to gather my strength before dealing with him.'

'He wants to make things up to you. He really means it . . . ' Before Calista could finish her sentence, Brook had pinned her to the bed and covered her lips with his.

'I am not interested in my father at the moment,' he said, when he finally raised his head. He still had her pinned to the bed. She could feel his breath against her cheek, and felt an uncontrollable desire to pull him closer to her. 'Only in the woman who has lain at my side for two days, and what she said about me to him.'

'He said he wanted to put you in a hospital.' Oh please do not let him have heard everything, she prayed silently. 'And I merely told him I would not allow it.'

'I heard that too.'

'Why did you not say you were awake?'

'It was such an interesting conversation I did not want to stop it.' While he spoke, he ran his hands over her body, sending delicious tremors down her spine. 'I learned so much.'

'You are not well,' she said. 'It would not be wise to exert yourself.'

'Then,' he said, kissing her between words, 'you . . . will . . . have . . . to

. . . be . . . very . . . very . . . gentle . . . with
. . . me.' Much to her regret he stopped
kissing her and became more serious.
'Because I have no intentions of allowing my father or anyone else to annul
this marriage.'

Calista had more or less come to the
same decision. 'I think you should at
least wait until you are well.'

'No. I have a feeling that by then you
will have found a way to avoid me.'

She stroked his cheek. 'No, I will not.
I promise I will not. I am here to stay
. . . for as long as you want me.'

'Forever it is then.' He enfolded her
in his arms, and despite her admittedly
half-hearted protestations, would not be
persuaded to rest.

'Are you alright?' she whispered several hours later. Her grey dress lay in a
heap on the floor, and she lay in a very
contented heap in Brook's arms. Even if
he did not love her, she had been left in
no doubt that he liked her very much.

'You have not succeeded in killing me
yet.'

'Oh do not joke about such things. Not after what happened.'

'Tell me that you love me,' he said drowsily.

'I love you.' She waited, longing and hoping he would say it in return. Even if he did not really mean it, in the sweet afterglow of their lovemaking she was quite happy to be lied to. But he was already fast asleep. She tried to content herself with his promise that they would be together forever. Surely it must mean he was fond of her, if nothing else.

14

Brook spent most of the morning sleeping, and Calista feared he might have a relapse. But by luncheon he insisted on getting dressed. Luncheon was then delayed somewhat by him deciding, whilst Calista was helping him to put on his shirt, that being undressed was much more pleasurable. She could not deny that he had a point.

In the afternoon, they received several visitors. The duke returned, along with Lady Bedlington, Evelyn and Mr. Benedict, who all naturally wanted to see how Brook fared. The latter three had all called in whilst he was unconscious, but there had been very little they could do for him other than allow him to rest and to heal. Calista also realized, with some embarrassment, that she might have been a little bit possessive about him and therefore given them the impression that their help was not needed.

They met in the drawing room, where Brook reclined on a chaise longue, looking more attractive than ever in a loose fitting white shirt and black breeches.

The duke seemed a little ill at ease to begin with, but everyone seemed to take their cue from Calista, who treated him as if he had always been a part of the circle, encouraging him to join in their conversations when he seemed to flag a little.

Evelyn had worrying news. 'Blanche went out yesterday morning and did not return.'

'Is it possible she has gone to the continent with Purbeck?' asked Brook. Calista had told him what his father discovered.

'That is what we thought,' said Evelyn. 'But then last night we received word that she had married.'

'Married? To whom?' asked Calista.

'You will not believe this. I can hardly believe it myself. As far as I am aware they have not spoken more than a couple of words to each other.'

'Not the King?' said Brook with a wry smile. 'I would not put it past Blanche, though she is not quite homely enough for his tastes.' Calista felt the familiar sting of jealousy, not much helped by him suggesting the Earl had 'homely' tastes. Was that how Brook saw her? Homely? Her feeling of envy was not much helped by her mild resentment that she was having to share him with others when she would much rather be alone with him. She realized she was being unreasonable, but her insecurity about his feelings for her overrode any other emotions. Not that she let anyone see how she felt. She was the perfect hostess, making sure they all had drinks.

'No, not the King,' said Evelyn, smiling sadly. 'The Earl of Garton.'

'What?' Calista almost dropped her cup of coffee.

'He's been on the lookout for a wife, as you know,' said Mr. Benedict. 'And I think when Blanche found out about what happened to Brook, she realized she might be implicated.'

'There is no proof of that,' said Evelyn, quickly.

'I am sure she would not have been,' said Brook.

'She managed to put herself in Garton's way,' said Mr. Benedict.

'I cannot decide whom I should wish more luck to,' said Lady Bedlington. 'Him or her. Oh, Evelyn, do not look like that. You know the girl is an absolute tartar. With any luck, she'll be just what Garton needs.'

Calista did not fancy the Earl of Garton's chances of living very long with Blanche as a wife, but she did not say so as she did not want to hurt Evelyn's feelings. Instead she looked under her lashes at Brook to try and ascertain how he had taken the news of Blanche's marriage. The information only served to remind her of how she came to be his wife. He had merely saved her from a bad situation, out of kindness and nobility.

That he desired her as a woman was without doubt, but she knew little of men, so did not know if they behaved differently when they were in love with a woman. Would his kisses be more ardent if he were with Blanche? It was hard to imagine how they could be, but she had to accept it was a possibility.

As Evelyn and Mr. Benedict made to leave, they had happier news for everyone. 'We are to be married,' said Mr. Benedict, putting his arm around Evelyn's shoulder. 'We hope that it will put right a wrong we did many years ago.'

Calista ran to kiss them both. 'I am so happy for you,' she said, unaccountably struck by sudden tears. She forced them back, not wanting to spoil Evelyn and Mr. Benedict's moment. 'I wish you a long and wonderful life together.'

'Thank you, dearest,' said Evelyn. 'I can marry much more contentedly knowing that you are now provided for.'

'I told you I would never hold you back.'

'I know that, dearest.'

'But as I've tried to tell Evelyn all along,' said Mr. Benedict, 'had you not been provided for, you would always have a home with us.'

'It is all academic now,' said Brook. 'We are very happy together, Calista and I. I can only wish you both the same joy.'

His words should have made Calista more content, but they only served to disturb her more. It was true they were happy together, but how long would that last when he grew tired of her in his bed? She put her feelings of pessimism down to tiredness. It had been a stressful few days, when she had not slept very well. And once Brook awoke, he gave her other reasons not to sleep. She suddenly longed for the privacy of a bedroom of her own and wondered how to broach the subject when the others had left.

'I think I may have an early night,' she said when they were alone. She could not look at him, so she stared into the fireplace.

'Yes, we will go up straight after dinner.'

'What I mean is that I'm very tired.'

'I see . . . Have I displeased you in any way?' What a question! He had certainly not displeased her, but she could feel herself being subsumed to his will again, and losing herself in the process.

'No, but you must be very tired too. You really have done too much since yesterday.'

'I would not have it any other way. Calista . . . '

'What?'

'Look at me.'

Reluctantly she turned around.

'I have said all along that I want us to have a proper marriage.'

'Yes, I know. But I am so tired and . . . '

'Then we will go to bed and sleep. That too is part of a proper marriage, is it not? Sleeping together in the same bed?'

'I do not think we will sleep.'

He smiled so seductively that she almost threw herself at him. 'If sleep is what you need, then sleep is what we shall do. You have my word of honour I shall not . . . bother you.' His lips curled up at the corners again.

She was the one to crumble first, having lain next to him for half an hour, trying to pretend she was not acutely aware of his presence beside her. She tried to make it seem casual, as if she were just checking to see if he still breathed by putting her hand on his chest. She did not fool him. He was already attuned to her moods.

'You are a very demanding woman,' he said with a grin, before gathering her up in his arms.

When she awoke, very late the following morning, Brook was not lying next to her. Panicking, she jumped out of bed and threw on her dressing gown. She had a sudden image of him having got up in the night and collapsed on his way to the bathroom, or perhaps even having fallen downstairs. The fact that the servants would most certainly had found him and let her know if the latter had happened, did not occur to her due to her overwhelming fear for his safety.

She rushed to the bathroom, but it was empty. She was just about to head to the staircase when she saw Brook coming out of the room that had once been the drawing room. 'There you are,' he said with a smile. He was fully dressed, looking refreshed and handsome.

'I was worried about you.'

'I'm sorry, I would have let you know, but you were very tired last night and I knew I should not be selfish and wake you again. As much as I wanted to.' His eyes moved over her body, and she was aware of not being nearly as well dressed as he was.

'I should go and get dressed.'

'Not yet. I have something I wanted to show you. The reason I got up early. I take it you have not seen this room yet.'

'Erm . . . no, the servants said that

only you had the key.'

'That is correct. I was going to surprise you with it on our wedding day, only events rather took over.' He held out his hand to her. 'Come, I have been spending the morning making sure everything is just right.'

To her surprise, when she reached him, he swept her up in his arms. 'This,' he said, 'is to make up for not carrying you over the threshold on our wedding day. And if I am honest, I prefer to do it now, as I show you this room. You inspired it.'

He carried her through the door, and she glanced around, her eyes widening in surprise and delight when she saw that he had created a magnificent library, just as she had suggested. The two walls had been knocked down, creating a room that was some one hundred feet long. 'Not quite as big as the library at Blenheim,' he said.

'Oh I do not mind. It is wonderful, wonderful! Put me down so I can take a proper look.'

'I am not sure I want to.'

'You can hardly carry me up and down the room. You are still not as well as you think you are.'

'Very well, I will put you down just this once.'

Calista practically skipped up and down the room, marvelling at the rows of books. Some were very old, whilst others were the latest editions of the most popular novels. The room had been furnished with plush sofas and chairs, with plenty of space for lounging and reading. Floor to ceiling sash windows let in the light so that it almost felt as though they were standing outside. The air was filled with the scent of dozens of vases of flowers.

'I had to replace all the original flowers,' Brook explained. 'Naturally they had not survived being locked up for several days. So that is what I wanted to do this morning, before you awoke.'

'Thank you, it's just ... oh, it's magnificent. Even better than I imagined it.'

'Nothing quite worked out as I wanted it to,' Brook said more seriously. He perched on the arm of one of the chairs.

'No, I realize that,' said Calista, feeling as if the light had gone out of the room. 'I know that you only ever meant to offer me your protection, but I will try and be a good wife to you. As you said, we are happy . . . '

Brook had jumped up from the arm of the chair, looking very angry. 'Protection? Who said so?'

'You did. When we were watching Evelyn and Mr. Benedict in the garden. You said you would protect me. And Blanche thought . . . '

'Blanche? Why does everything always come down to that witch? You thought I offered you my protection? That I was asking you to be my mistress?'

'Were you not?'

'No, I damn well was not.'

'Oh, then if I misunderstood . . . '

'You most certainly did. What sort of man do you take me for?'

'I . . . '

'Good God. No wonder you seemed so upset to be marrying me, if you think I am the sort of man who would ask an innocent girl of twenty to be his mistress. Is that how I appear to you?'

'No, of course not.'

'I hoped, Calista, I hoped against hope that once we were married you might come to love me. But how could you ever love me, believing such a thing? Dammit, Calista!'

She wanted to tell him that she did love him, only she was not yet sure enough of him. 'Why should it matter if I love you or not?'

'Do you really have to ask that? Why else would I step in and stop you from marrying that oaf Garton? I could not bear to think of him touching you. Believe me when I say I was ready to kill him for even thinking it.'

'I thought you only married me to be noble and kind. I thought you loved Blanche, because she is so much more beautiful than I am.'

'Blanche!' He laughed bitterly. 'I would no more let that woman in my life than I would a viper. Oh she set her cap at me, until she realized she might have bigger fish to fry, but I am not as stupid as young Purbeck. Or perhaps I am an even bigger fool.'

'What do you mean?'

'I was going to propose to you in this room, until events overtook us. I know that most women like to be proposed to in a garden, but I thought this was more suited to you. I was going to fill it with flowers, at least to make it seem a bit like a garden, then bring you here and say everything to you that I know women like to hear . . . '

'No . . . '

'I see. You do not want to hear it. Then I am sorry I have wasted my time.'

'No, Brook. I do not want you to say what you think I want to hear. I just want you to say what is in your heart.'

'Why, have I not made a big enough fool of myself?'

'No. I mean, you're not a fool. I was wrong about you offering me your protection, and I am sorry, but it never occurred to me that you would ever feel for me what I feel for you.' She knew she was going to have to be brave again. Even if it meant him laughing in her face. 'I love you. I've always loved you, but I thought you only married me to save me from Garton and I was afraid that if I told you how I felt, it would make you feel more responsible for me. I wanted to give you a chance to escape . . .'

'Escape?' Brook had crossed the room without her realizing. He pulled her into his arms. 'Don't you know that I've been in your captivity since the first day I met you? I don't want to escape. I love you, Calista. I have loved you from the moment I opened the carriage door and saw your brave, beautiful face glaring at me, determined to face your attacker head on. That was the woman I fell in love with. The same woman who stood up to my father.' He stroked her hair. 'I think that you have been so overshadowed by Blanche's personality all these years, so convinced that she is better than you, that you really have no idea how much more beautiful you are.'

He loved her! It was all she had ever wanted to hear. 'You said that the Earl of Garton's taste was for homely women.'

'You did not see his first wife . . . '

'But he wanted to marry me.'

'Then he showed some rare good taste.'

'That was very well saved,' said Calista, with a wicked grin, 'but I know what you said about him preferring homely women.'

'Well, perhaps you do give off a homely air sometimes, with that innocent face of yours.' He kissed her neck and laughed softly. 'But he has not seen you as I've seen you.'

She blushed and hid her head in his shoulder. Despite how intimate they had been over the past couple of days, she suddenly felt as if everything between them was brand new, even the intimacy. 'I'm glad you saved me from him,' she whispered. 'I could not bear to think . . . '

Brook held her closer still, and she was aware of his lips tightening. 'No, neither can I, so do not even think of it. You're mine, and I promise I will protect you. Not in the disgusting way you thought, but as my wife, as my love.'

'And I'll protect you too.'

'I have no doubt about that, my little Boadicea.'

THE END